The Denial

Also by Ross Clark

The Denial

Ross Clark

LUME BOOKS

LUME BOOKS

First published in 2020 by Lume Books
30 Great Guildford Street,
Borough, SE1 0HS

ISBN 978-1-83901-210-5

Typeset using Atomik ePublisher from Easypress Technologies

www.lumebooks.co.uk

About the Author

Born in Worcester in 1966, Ross Clark was educated in east Kent and at Trinity Hall, Cambridge. He won The Spectator Young Writers Award in 1989 and has since worked extensively as a journalist, his work appearing in *The Daily Telegraph*, *The Spectator*, *The Times* and many other publications. He is also the author of several books, including *The Great Before*, a satire on the pessimism of the green movement, *How to Label a Goat*, *The Road to Southend Pier* and *A Broom Cupboard of One's Own*, and a musical, *The White Feather*.

With thanks to James Dent, for help with the meteorology, and to my wife, Catherine, for her insights

1

On hearing that strong northerly winds had been forecast for Guy Fawkes Night, Bryan Geavis was in a quandary as to how to spend the last hours of daylight. Should he secure the climbing roses on the front of his house, or should he retire upstairs to follow the storm on the internet?

Roses were a passion of his – he had notebooks in which he had registered the date they had flowered, stretching back 40 years. Yet he found something uniquely seductive about a North Sea storm. He loved watching the satellite images of the swirling masses of cloud as they raced, usually from west to east, stirring up a seemingly innocuous body of grey water into lethal rage. Compared with the Atlantic, the North Sea was not so much a tea cup as the saucer – so much shallower than some of the fjords and lochs which fed into it, and yet prone to swells and surges which could surprise shipping and on occasion snap the legs of an oil platform.

Storms had once been Geavis' profession. He had spent three decades as a meteorologist on oil platforms, the lives of divers and drilling engineers dependent on his ability to detect and predict the path of a brewing storm. He had an innate sense of how to translate the isobars on a map into the real effects – he knew how winds would snatch at anything that had not been lashed down, how a rogue wave could wash a man off a platform if he was not secured with a line. It had been his judgement, his responsibility, to tell whether or not outside work would be possible on the platforms from day to day.

He had carried on doing this for over 30 years, until a corporate restructuring at Albion Oil had eliminated his job, and he had been unwillingly sent ashore to spend a few anticlimactic years in the company's PR department. As soon as he had been free to take his pension, he had done so – and in retirement reverted to storm-watching as a hobby. Friends occasionally called him an oddball for it. He was ribbed on the occasion, during a family Christmas, when he had excused himself from the festivities because he wanted to check on the progress of a frontal system.

"Bryan, it's not normal to invite people around, then disappear upstairs because you want to watch a storm," his wife, Olivia, had told him. But it was not going to make any difference. He loved storms, and was not going to be deflected from his interest.

Inevitably, it was the storm that won the battle for his affections on Guy Fawkes Night. He hastily bound his roses as best he could, then retired upstairs to his computer screen. What he saw immediately disturbed him.

For two days, a storm had been stuck in the middle of the North Sea, drawing cold winds down from the north over the whole of Britain. The 6.00 pm weather forecast by the Agency for Modelling Climate Chaos (formerly the Met Office) had predicted that the storm would start wandering towards the east coast overnight and deepen a little, tightening the isobars and strengthening the winds. Instead, it seemed to be sinking southwards towards the Thames Estuary – straight for Geavis' own house. Worse, it was deepening more quickly than the Agency had suggested.

Geavis knew at once what it meant. Already, the seas were high: two days of northerly winds in the North Sea had funnelled water southwards – a classic tidal surge. But it was about to get a lot worse. Geavis checked the tide tables, which confirmed his fears. At the storm's current rate of progress the northern flank of the storm, with its easterly winds, would align with the estuary at around midnight – just in time for the 00:24 hours spring tide. Anyone relying on the television weather forecast would be entirely unprepared for the almost certain flooding that was to come.

His brain raced. People could die, and he was in a position to do something about it. He felt had to act, but how?

He called his wife to come downstairs. "Olivia, Olivia! Look at this!"

She did him the courtesy of coming to have a look, but she did not really know what she was looking at. "There's a big ball of fluff over the

North Sea," she said. "But how do you know it is coming this way?" When he explained his thinking, still she was unconvinced. "Surely it could still miss us, as they said on the telly?"

"No, no," said Geavis, becoming agitated. "I've seen enough of these to know what I am looking at. It's coming this way, alright. This could be devastation."

"But there's nothing about it on the news. Wouldn't they be saying?"

"They can't have seen the storm turn our way. Their models are wrong."

The danger was disturbingly close. Floodwaters whipped up by the storm would not reach Geavis' own house, which, as he had taken care to establish when he bought it, was at 37 feet above mean sea level. But walk a few streets southwards and the land dipped, as Essex met the sea. For those who lived on the seafront, only the bulwark of a concrete sea wall would protect them from the storm surge. And tonight, that wall was in danger of being overtopped.

If that happened, residents would have little warning. The water would spill, slowly at first, then in a great rush. The water would keep on coming, and coming, rising 10 feet in a minute or two. For the occupants of the bungalows – and they mostly were bungalows, on the seafront – there would be nowhere to go.

In his mind, Geavis was already running up and down the seafront with a loudhailer. "Danger, danger! Evacuate your homes at once! There is an acute flood risk at high tide tonight!"

But in reality, he had no loudhailer.

Instead, he made a call to the local radio station. A producer listened, and said he would raise the matter with the station's weather forecaster. Geavis tuned in, and half an hour later was at first flattered to be mentioned – only to hear his warning dismissed.

"Apparently, a listener called in earlier to say that there is a severe storm heading directly for Essex," came the forecast. "Well, don't worry unduly. The information we have at the moment is that the worst of the winds will pass us by. We'll keep you informed if the picture changes." And then they played an old hit, 'Riders on the Storm' by The Doors.

"They're taking the mickey!" said Geavis.

He went down to dinner asking himself: had it been enough? Had he done all he possibly could?

*

"You're not still worried about that storm?" asked Olivia, sensing his disquiet.

"It's the speed it's coming down the east coast," he said. "That's absolutely crucial. I'm going to have another look in a minute, but they're going to be sitting ducks, everyone who lives in low-lying places along the Thames."

"If it's going to be rough weather the very least you can do is get a good meal inside you. Honestly, the efforts I make – and you never comment."

Geavis grunted, but he couldn't bring himself to lie – it wasn't a good meal, and it would hurt his pride to say so. He couldn't overcome the disappointment he felt at every mealtime. How he missed meat! The jars of vitamins and mineral supplements that Olivia always put on the table before him said it all – why did he need those if sustainable food (as it was always described on the packaging) was as healthy as everyone kept telling him it was? Maybe he was wrong, maybe vegan food *was* as good for him as it was for the planet; yet he couldn't help feeling from the pit of his unfulfilled stomach that it wasn't properly sustaining him. What irritated him most was the way that his dinner had been dressed up as a steak, as if disguising a concoction of beetroot would be enough to stave off his cravings for the real thing.

"They're not too bad, are they, these steaks?" said Olivia.

Geavis wanted to speak his mind, but he knew it would hurt and besides, he'd said it often enough before – he just wanted a real steak. Or some chunks, or some mince.

But what hope did he have? There was no absolute ban on eating meat, but in practice it had become difficult for ordinary folk to procure it – or indeed any food officially labelled as 'unsustainable'. Every citizen had to submit quarterly carbon audits, accounting for the carbon emissions for which they were personally responsible. The allowances were so tight there was little room for meat and in any case, public disapproval was heaped upon those who attempted to eat it.

12

The last time Olivia had tried to buy a couple of steaks, about three years earlier, she had been surrounded by several people tut-tutting at her choice. "You're killing the planet, you effing moron!" she was told. Embarrassed and feeling threatened, Olivia had put the steaks back and had never tried to buy meat since.

It was possible to be prescribed meat for medical reasons, or to be put in touch with a specialist supplier if you could prove you had a religious need. But few butchers would dare set up a shop or market stall to supply the general public, now. Any such establishment would quickly be surrounded by a mob of wailing activists – popularly known as the Greenshirts – who would hold a symbolic funeral for the dead animals and threaten to put the trader before the courts on a charge of animal cruelty. Country people were known illicitly to snare rabbits and other creatures. But for most people, the only option was to down the officially approved vegan food and keep on popping the vitamin pills.

Geavis pushed his half-empty plate away from him and announced that was going to take a walk down to the seafront.

"But what about the waves?" said Olivia. "You said it was going to be dangerous."

"And that is exactly why I've got to go"

He pulled on a set of waterproofs – garments he had once worn on the oil platforms – and opened the door carefully. Even so, he was surprised at how it was snatched by a gust of wind. The winds were not yet gale force, but they were heading that way. He was sure that he felt the cold more than he had in the old days, and he was convinced it was because he didn't have a good meal inside him. A branch of one of his roses had become detached, which scratched his face, but he hadn't the time to deal with it. Rain was now falling almost horizontally, and dark puddles were forming on the pavement. He couldn't seem to help scooping rainwater into his shoes.

With each street, the wind seemed to strengthen until, just short of the seafront, he found himself having to cling to fence posts just as he used to cling to the rails of the oil platforms. The house names – Sunny Bank, Sunnyside, Fair View – were laughably at odds with the evening's reality.

When he reached the sea wall, he gripped it with both hands and looked

13

over. At low tide, the sea could be half a mile away. But the water was coming up fast and the last few patches of muddy sand were disappearing. Another hour and the waters would be up to where he was standing. He looked back, down into the tidy, ornament-filled gardens of the first row of bungalows. They were lightweight buildings and would be reduced to matchsticks if the waves reached them.

He tried to imagine what it would look like if the wall failed to hold the water back: a mass of tangled chairs, concrete frogs and maidens, plant pots and garden chairs, all mixed with detritus brought over with the water – land and sea suddenly and ferociously mixed together.

Had he time to warn everyone of what was coming? He did the calculations in his head. There must be 120 properties in the line of danger, he estimated. Even if he spent just a minute at each, trying to explain what was going to happen he would hardly have time to reach them all. But supposing he instructed his first randomly selected resident to go and warn two neighbours, and to ask each of them to warn two others? The mathematics of this appealed to him: two, four, eight, 16, 32. The job of warning everyone could be done inside 10 minutes. As he walked towards the first property, a quick flash of a thought passed through his mind: he could be the hero of the hour.

At the first bungalow, there was a light on and the sound of a television in the front room, yet still it took several knocks to rouse the woman inside. She then took up more vital seconds as she decided whether or not to open the door. She sized him up through the glass: who was he, and what did he want this time of night? Eventually she did open the door, but only on its chain.

"Excuse me for disturbing you," said Geavis. "But I am a retired meteorologist who lives in the neighbourhood and I am convinced that a storm is coming our way. The weather forecasters have underestimated the danger. There is a serious flood risk and you need to leave your home."

He could see it in her face – she was trying to work out his true motive. Was it a distraction burglary? Was he going to attack her, even if he didn't look a threatening type? What has happened to the community, he thought, that neighbours can't trust each other?

She thought much the same.

"But where would I go?" she asked. "It isn't like the old days, when I could have jumped in the car and gone and stayed with Daisy for the night. I can't go out in this."

"And you can't stay in, either."

She went to look for her cat but made no commitment to follow his instruction. He moved on.

At the next house, a couple were more open to being persuaded to leave, but they insisted in going up to the sea wall themselves to have a look at the waters. Already, the sea was a couple of feet higher than when Geavis had first looked; water was now slapping up against the concrete, sending spray and foam over the top of the wall.

"You're right, it does look high," one of them said. Yet it was still hard to convince them of the danger they faced.

Geavis had only managed to visit a couple more houses before he heard doors up and down the street beginning to open. Almost simultaneously. he heard a siren. Then another. There were blue flashing lights. Then came a voice, over a loudhailer.

"Warning of severe risk to life," came the words. "We're evacuating this street. Please leave at once."

Geavis' phone began to bleep. He looked and saw the same message. It had picked up his location and was sending him a personal warning.

Out of nowhere, an emergency flood plan was swinging into action. Residents appeared at doorways, hastily doing up their children's coats. Some carried pets and assorted possessions – stuff they ought to have left behind. Geavis felt relieved. The responsibility was no longer his. He could return home – which he did, grabbing at lampposts and bushes as he went. The wind was now stronger, and by the time he reached home he felt exhausted just from battling against it.

He was surprised by Olivia's reaction when he got inside. It hadn't occurred to him that she would be cross.

"For Christ's sake, don't you ever do that to me again," she said. "It's utterly foolish to go out in that weather. Couldn't you even have rung me? So typical of you not to think of me."

He didn't know whether to apologise or explain. He couldn't engage with Olivia's anger – his mind was full of the weather.

"They've caught up," he said. "They spotted the storm, after all. They've evacuated three streets. Everyone's going to the leisure centre."

Sleep was out of the question. Geavis retreated to his study and followed the storm, the eye of which was now spinning quickly down the East Anglian coast. On its northern flank the winds were not only strengthening; they were beginning to align with the Thames, which would serve to push a bulge of water westwards towards London, rising ever higher as the river narrowed. He sat by the window, looking out for floodwaters, and watching the odd limp firework in the distance.

As the high tide approached it became agonising for him not to know whether the sea wall had held. He stayed in, listening to the radio and to the winds as they ruffled his roof tiles. But at 2.30 in the morning, with Olivia asleep, his curiosity became too great. He let himself out of the house and made his way towards the sea.

Two streets away, he came up against a police cordon and an officer on patrol.

"Not through here, sir," said the officer when he saw him. "Flood protection."

"But the tide is receding now."

"Doesn't make any difference. No-one is allowed – not even if you live in these streets. Gather at the leisure centre and we'll let you back in the morning, with any luck."

Geavis turned away, but then wished he had had it out with the officer. What was the point in keeping the streets closed now? It was just authorities trying to make up for their failure to see the storm earlier – people covering their backsides, that was what it was.

Geavis tried an alternative road down to the sea, but found that shut off too. Then, he remembered a little alleyway and found that the police had forgotten to close it. He walked fast along there, downhill past rotting garages still sheltering long-disused cars. He kept looking out for the floodwaters he felt sure would be there. Would they have reached the first street, the second street or the promenade?

But he didn't find any floodwaters, other than large puddles on the seafront, little seas with islands of pebbles. They weren't deep and he guessed they had been caused by spray, not by water pouring over the flood wall. The defences had held.

He peered over and saw the tide receding. The emergency was over and everything was looking normal – except for a layer of weed encrusted onto the wall, a few inches from the top, which served as evidence of how close the sea had come to breaching the defences. Having worked himself into the expectation of a major disaster he couldn't help but feel, perversely, a little disappointed – an emotion he tried to dismiss as he turned for home and his bed.

*

The following morning, he was awoken by Olivia.

"There's been devastation in London," she said. "It's the only thing they're talking about on the radio."

The tide had surged up the Thames until it ran headlong into floodwaters draining from the heavy rainfall that had fallen in southern England in recent weeks. In several places the river defences had been breached, and there had been casualties.

It would not be clear how many had died until emergency services had visited the flooded properties, but reports were already trickling through. An elderly man had been found drowned in Woolwich. A couple had died trying to save a dog in Beckton. A tree had fallen on a house in Leyton; crushing a couple in bed. Several cars had been found on the river's foreshore, having been swept off nearby streets. At least one motorist was dead, though not all vehicles had yet been checked. A youth had been severely injured when the firework he had just lit was blown over by the wind and fired itself into his chest.

Worst of all, there were reports of a major incident in Deptford, details of which were sketchy, but many deaths were feared.

The secretary of state for the climate emergency, Sarah Downwood, gave a statement.

17

"London was hit last night by one of the worst storms of the past century. My thoughts go out to those who have been affected by the disaster, the full extent of which is only becoming clear with daylight. It is yet another sharp reminder that the climate emergency is not some abstract problem for the distant future. It is with us in the here and now."

There was a flurry of questions from reporters.

"Can you tell us why the storm was not forecast?"

"Please understand that we are in an emergency situation," replied Downwood. "Our thoughts at the moment are with the victims of this disaster. I will make further statements later, but that is all I will be saying for now, thank you."

Then a reporter asked the question that had just occurred to Geavis himself.

"Was the barrier closed? And if not, why not?"

But Downwood gave no answer.

"Of all the things!" said Geavis. "They didn't even close the Thames Barrier! That was the whole point of it: to save London from a night like this!"

To Olivia, whose career was in medicine, rivers and tides meant little. But she then asked a question which had not occurred to Geavis.

"What about Adam?"

Adam was their son. He lived with his partner and daughter in a flat several streets back from the river in Beckton – a ground floor flat.

"Surely they would have been out of harm's way?" he said. But the more he thought about it, the less sure he was. Did the land rise or fall between their flat and the river? He tried to think it over, attempting to recall the lie of the land from his visits there, then resorted to his computer to find out.

Locating the flat by satellite image, he discovered it stood just a metre above the usual high-water mark of the Thames, and possibly two metres below the level of the previous night's tidal surge.

If the river's flood wall had been breached, Adam and his family would have been submerged. They might not even have realised the danger they were in.

He kept this horrible realisation from Olivia.

Olivia, meanwhile, was already ringing her son – or trying to. There was no answer. She tried Chloe. Still no answer.

What about Amber, their 10-year-old daughter? Surely *she* must answer – she never seemed to put her phone down. But from Amber, too, there was no answer.

Might they just be busy? Geavis found himself visualising a wall of water bursting into the family's flat. There was only one thing for it. They were not going to rest until they had gone to Beckton and satisfied themselves that all were safe.

But how to get there? Olivia did as she always did when they needed to make a journey outside their immediate neighbourhood – although that had happened less and less in recent years. She tried to call up an electropod via her phone. These autonomous egg-shaped vehicles were supposed to arrive within minutes, but in practice this was rare. There were not enough electropods to meet demand, and they were prone to malfunction. Some had been stolen and illicitly reprogrammed for the thief's exclusive use. When complaints were made to the mayor, his answer was always the same: electropods were there to be used by everyone, now and then, but they were never supposed to be a substitute for private cars.

Meanwhile, most cars had been removed from the road. Even electric cars were proving incompatible with the ever-tighter carbon budgets being placed on individuals. Not only that, a shortage of rare metals had stalled production of batteries.

"We all need to ask ourselves whether we really need to travel so much," was the mayor's standard response.

While waiting for the electropod, Geavis and Olivia continued to ring their family members, but without success. They kept the radio on. More details of the storm were emerging. Several more bodies had been discovered: the death toll was now 24. It was being reported that the authorities had attempted to close the barrier, but by the time they realised the need the currents had been too strong. Pressure was building on Sarah Downwood, who was being accused of being far too laid-back. Several residents of districts close to the river claimed they had not received sufficient warning.

"The first I knew there was a storm was when water started pouring in my living room through the cat flap," one lady in Dagenham complained. "It was only after that I had a telephone call warning me there was a flood on the way. What use is that?"

Her words were played over and over again on every news bulletin. By 10:30 am , Sarah Downwood was forced to make another appearance before the cameras.

"Further to my earlier statement, let me assure you that the government will do all it can to ensure that this will never happen again. I am well aware of claims that this weather event was not forecast as early as it might have been. But we all have to be aware that severe weather events like these are becoming ever more common. It is a stark reminder of the climate emergency we face and the drastic measures we need to take."

While some reporters approved, others were unconvinced that she was doing enough. The subject of the non-closure of the barrier wouldn't go away. Another question was now being asked: will there be a public inquiry?

Feeling under pressure, Downwood raised her arms and made an instant decision, which horrified her civil servants.

"Yes. I assure you there will be."

Geavis nodded approvingly. "If they didn't close that barrier, that's negligence," he said. "Heads must roll."

Half an hour later the electropod had still not arrived.

"We could have walked to the station by now," said Olivia, before suggesting they did just that.

A few hundred yards down the road they discovered why their electropod had not arrived: there it was, buzzing with strained effort as it tried repeatedly, but without success, to mount a pile of earth, gravel and other detritus washed into the road by the previous night's rain.

"Is that ours?" asked Olivia.

"I'm not getting in it now," replied Geavis. "Pathetic things!"

It was a mile and a half walk to the station. There were few people about, and little traffic. Several people were undertaking makeshift repairs to their homes, securing flaps of roofing felt loosened by the high winds. The air was strangely calm, given how recently the storm had passed.

Yet, the peace was broken by the sound of an aeroplane. Aeroplanes always caught Geavis' attention. Where once they had been ubiquitous, now they were such a rarity that it was difficult to ignore them. He found himself asking: who can that be, flying when most of us don't even get to travel by car?

As with meat, as with cars, there was no specific law against flying, yet it was an experience that had become impossible for most people. Their carbon allowances were not generous enough to allow them to take foreign holidays anymore, such as they had enjoyed in their youth. To fly, it was necessary either to cut down the rest of your carbon emissions to virtually zero, or otherwise to obtain a special permit, for which you had to plead some desperate need to travel. The death of a close relative might do the trick, as would, on occasions, a cultural or religious need – the Executive for Personal Carbon Budgeting could sometimes take a generous view on that. But holidays were out of the question. Unless, that is, you were one of the chosen few who qualified for a much more generous carbon allowance.

Looking up at the plane, Geavis could easily guess who was inside. "Bloody climate influencers!" he said. "While people are drowning down here, they are up there watching!"

To become a climate influencer – or CI, for short – was the ambition of almost everyone. It opened doors, brought privileges of which others could only dream. The CIs enjoyed much higher carbon allowances because, it was argued, they needed to reach the widest possible audience in order to spread their message. They had to reach conferences and attend other events around the world. They needed to make speeches and share their wisdom with public administrators, especially in tropical regions where, they believed, people often seemed especially resistant to understanding the climate emergency and the need to curtail their lifestyles for the sake of the climate.

As one of the most prominent CIs, an actress-turned-campaigner by the name of Zoe Fluff, had put it on the radio the previous week: "Our hardest work is in some of those remote communities where people just stare at you when you suggest that by burning parts of the forest they are fouling their own environment and changing the weather. They don't see the connection. But with persistence, you can get through to them. Spend time working with people in their forests and on their beaches, and eventually they accept that what they have been doing is wrong and they must change their ways. It is such a beautiful moment when you realise your message is finally hitting home."

A CI found it much easier to own a car, too. While there was no general ban on car ownership, for a non-CI to own a car would almost certainly result in an illegally high carbon footprint. Without a CI sticker on the windscreen, cars were liable to be pulled over by the police and the driver suspected of evading the carbon allowance system.

Sometimes, activists would surround a private car, or lie in front of it and invite the driver to run them over if he dared. But of course, he wouldn't dare. Usually, the motorist would be shamed into submission, and would emerge tearfully from his vehicle, to be comforted by the crowd as he confessed to his selfishness.

Geavis and Olivia arrived at the station to find there were no trains; the overhead wires had been brought down in several places by the winds. If they were going to reach Beckton they would have to walk.

Although daunted by the thought of making the journey on foot, Geavis found himself enjoying it. Once-choked highways now carried little traffic. The freshness of the air was a blessing for anyone who remembered the old days. But Olivia was complaining about her knees, and the peace was suddenly shattered by a fast-moving car which caught them unawares and had to swerve to avoid them, hooting as it went.

"Bloody CIs!" said Olivia. "Why do they have to be so selfish?"

The encounter with the car seemed to provoke a change in their mood. The more they tried to convince themselves that their son and his family were okay, the darker became the thoughts that gathered at the back of their minds.

"If there were floodwaters in the streets in front of their flat, surely there would have been a commotion," said Olivia. "They couldn't have slept through that. They would have got up and saved themselves."

Geavis was silent for a moment, then said: "But their flat is on the wrong side of the building. Would they have heard anything?"

"If they evacuated their flat in a hurry, they could have forgotten their phones. Or dropped them if they waded through water. That might explain their silence."

"Didn't they say on the news that a woman had been found drowned in Beckton?"

"Would that have been the same part?"

"Beckton isn't that big. If it floods in one place it would have flooded in another."

"Amber can't swim!"

"That might not have made a difference – the water would have been so cold anyone could have died of shock."

Geavis hated to look at his phone but couldn't resist it any longer. The reception was poor, but he just made out a headline: "Thousands Unaccounted For."

"Don't say this is happening!"

*

Over the course of their three-hour walk, Geavis and Olivia gradually became convinced their family had drowned. That son, daughter-in-law and granddaughter had made a heroic effort, but it hadn't been enough. Perhaps they had become separated. Maybe Amber had got into trouble and her parents stopped to help. Or the other way around. It would have been typical of them, to have given up their own chance to escape by stopping to help others…

Geavis' mind raced on; he couldn't stop it. Would he have to give a eulogy at the funeral? What would he say? Would they set up a tribute page on social media for Amber? It was what she would have wanted. Surely she would have many online friends desperate to know what had happened to her?

They arrived at Beckton to find the streets six inches deep in water in some places, and dry elsewhere. The water must have been a little deeper at some point, because Adam's doormat had been displaced by several feet – presumably lifted up by the floodwaters. But there was no water inside the flat, and in any case it turned out the family would not have been drowned if the water *had* come in – someone had knocked on their door, warning of the rising water, and they spent the next few hours at the top of the communal staircase in their block before returning home as the water fell.

They were fine.

"Sorry that you were so worried," said Adam, "but the electricity has been off and our phones have run down. How else could we have contacted you?"

Geavis felt relieved, but at the same time foolish. "Why didn't we think of that?" he asked Olivia. "So obvious, that there would be no electricity."

"And why didn't you and your meteorologist friends see it coming?" said Adam.

There was a mischievous look in his eye, suggesting he wasn't really expecting a serious answer from his father, but Geavis couldn't help taking it as an attack on his professional pride. He felt defensive of his former colleagues, and explained how forecasts could sometimes go hopelessly wrong. He started to talk about how the mathematical models meteorologists created of the atmosphere worked; how sometimes they predicted what would happen with great accuracy but how on other occasions one small detail threw the whole forecast awry. That is what had happened the previous night: the storm had veered off in a different direction than that predicted.

"Nine times out of ten we can get it right," he said. "And hardly anyone notices, let alone praises us. But when things start to go wrong, they go very wrong, very quickly. The errors feed off themselves. It's chaos."

"It certainly was chaos round here last night," said Adam. "Your old colleagues chose a bad night to get it wrong."

"That's not quite what I meant by chaos. I meant chaotic mathematically. It's the reason why we can't predict the weather more than a few days ahead – and sometimes not beyond a few hours."

Amber, who had been drawing yet listening intently, was interested by this idea. "But we know what the weather is going to be like in 100 years' time. There's going to be bigger storms and more droughts."

"You're talking about the climate," said Geavis. "That's not quite the same as the weather. No-one knows if it is going to be sunny or rainy a hundred years from today, but we think it might, on average, be warmer then than it is today."

24

"We *think* it is going to be warmer? Don't we *know?*"

"We think we know. If we are right that the rise in temperatures is being forced by the level of carbon dioxide in the atmosphere then, yes, the Earth is likely to keep on getting warmer. But the trouble is, there are a lot of things we don't know about the climate, so I'm afraid we can never really be sure what will happen. Temperatures have risen and fallen sharply in the past, without human influence, and for reasons we don't fully understand. There is always an outside chance we have got it all wrong and the climate could get cooler."

"Cooler?" said Amber. Her grandfather's answer struck her as unsatisfactory, but she couldn't quite tell why. She was used to being given answers, and he couldn't give her any.

She went back to her drawing and decided to leave the matter until another time.

2

Just as the floodwaters had risen, peaked and then receded, so too did the projected death toll. At Friday lunchtime there were reports of possibly 10,000 people lost "…and who knows how many more have not yet even been reported missing?" the newscaster rhetorically asked. "The population of the boroughs affected runs into the hundreds of thousands."

The leader of the opposition, Jake Raglan, declared it to be "possibly the greatest natural disaster ever to strike this country. Except it isn't natural at all. It is an unnatural disaster, caused by human hands."

But that afternoon, with communications restored, the people who had been missed began to make contact with those who had been missing them. Flooded homes and cars had been searched and mostly found empty. The estimated death toll began to fall, firstly into the low thousands, then into the high hundreds and then the low hundreds. By the following Monday, when the flooded basement of the House of Commons had been pumped out and a debate was hastily called to discuss the disaster, the toll was beginning to congeal at around 35 – a figure with which MPs who had written speeches on the presumption that thousands were dead struggled to contend.

"This disaster changes everything," said a tearful MP for an east London seat. "Never have so many in this country died from the consequences of our own selfishness. We must now accept that the reality of the climate crisis is hitting us far harder, in a far more deadly way than any of us could have imagined even just a few months ago."

Jake Raglan, fearful that another MP was stealing his thunder, upped his rhetoric. "It is now an all-out struggle for survival in which every single one of us must be engaged. The government's complacency in this has verged on the criminal. It must now explain what it is going to do."

Geavis imagined himself in the chamber, responding to this. He wanted to put Raglan right. The death toll, he wanted to say, was not as high as that of the great North Sea tidal surge of 1953, still less that of the great storm of 1703. He found himself a little angry when Sarah Downwood responded to Raglan's remarks without acknowledging this fact.

"I assure the right honourable gentleman that we are not asleep on the job. The whole country is deeply shocked by what has happened. I am today taking measures that will further reduce our contribution to climate devastation. This government's target for achieving net zero carbon emissions will be brought forward by a further two years. With this is mind, I am cutting the personal carbon allowance by a further 10 percent. Climate influencers will, for now, be exempt from any cut, though this will be reviewed at a later date. "

Raglan stood up and immediately demanded that she make it a 20 percent cut.

*

The deaths reported presented a varied picture of misfortune. Several people had been caught in basement flats, perhaps unaware of any imminent hazard until water began to pour in through windows and doors. There was a homeless man who had taken to sleeping halfway up a flight of concrete steps adjacent to the river: he may have been the first victim. A couple had died when their houseboat was torn from its moorings and overturned, tipping them into the floodwaters. A man had died, it was believed, while trying to save a trapped dog – the animal survived but the man collapsed from a heart attack. A disorientated motorist driving on a flooded street had lost his bearings and driven into the river.

But the single biggest loss of life, and the case that came to grab most public attention, had occurred in an underground garage close to the river in Deptford. It wasn't clear what had been going on – some suggested a party, others an orgy or some kind of pagan ritual – but whatever it was, around 100 people had failed to hear or take notice of a flood warning and found themselves trapped.

In their panic to escape, some had fallen and been trampled. A dozen bodies had been recovered. There were more questions at this stage than there were facts. How had they failed to take notice of a flood warning that had been broadcast an hour before high tide, when they could have calmly walked out of the basement? Everyone else in the immediate area had made themselves safe, so why not the revellers? While some suggested that the music must have drowned out the sirens, speculation began to circulate on the internet and in newspapers that drugs were involved.

"They want us all to feel guilty for the flood deaths," wrote Tyra Gaunt, a columnist on the *Daily Torrent* whose name had become a byword for causing offence. "But, sorry, I'm not going to shed tears over a bunch of junkies too off their heads to hear a loud and audible flood warning."

The response to her column was, as she expected and privately hoped, swift and outraged. There were calls for her to be sacked – a regular backdrop to her working life – but they seemed to be amplified beyond what was usual. For a day or two, Gaunt's column became the lead news story, distracting from coverage of the flood itself. A petition was begun to "silence the haters for good," demanding not just her dismissal from the newspaper but also her prosecution under laws against hate speech. An angry crowd gathered outside the newspaper's offices with banners. "Killed by climate hell, and now their reputations murdered," read one. The editor of the *Daily Torrent* held out for five days, defending his columnist, until Lady Smithers, the wife of the proprietor, was spotted and harangued as she alighted from a taxi outside Harrods. Within hours, Tyra Gaunt was dismissed.

She took the news from her editor with incredulity. "But I was doing what you wanted me to do, wasn't I?"

She sloped off down the street, feeling angry, cheated, yet with an uncomfortable thought inside her head: having trained her fire on individuals and institutions every week for quarter of a century shouldn't she be a little more accepting now that the guns had been turned on her? It didn't stop her calling the editor from home and threatening a lawsuit if she was not reinstated, but in the event it was Tyra herself who narrowly escaped being charged with public order offences.

The Tyra Gaunt affair served to concentrate attention on the Deptford victims. A week after the disaster, the road outside the apartment block where the disaster had occurred had become taken over by a shrine of flowers and other objects. A vigil was held. The victims became the face of the disaster, not so much pitied as exalted. Few, after Tyra Gaunt, dared speak ill of them, even in private. It turned out they had broken into the basement without permission, and had been holding a ceremony to heal the Earth from humankind's evils, involving the sacrifice of a motor-car, parts of which were found strewn around the basement. Loud music and, yes, drugs had been involved too. But who was to judge them when it was clear the flood warnings should have been louder?

"How ironic," said the mayor of London, calling by to visit the scene, "that these beautiful people were meeting to express their deep love for the Earth – and were overwhelmed by a man-made storm".

That idea irritated Bryan Geavis. Of course it wasn't a man-made storm, he muttered to himself. You can't make a storm. But he had something else on his mind. He needed to submit his quarterly carbon return to the Executive for Personal Carbon Budgeting, and was struggling with the figures, not least because he wasn't sure on which date the 10 percent reduction in the personal carbon allowance had kicked in. No-one seemed to know. He searched online, made phone calls, even read through what Ms Downwood had said in parliament, all to no avail.

The quarterly carbon return was required of all citizens. Itinerant people could generally escape it, but for everyone else it had become a never-ending chore. Most people paid for a carbon assessor to do the work for them, at some cost. Those who took this option needed only to supply the assessor with their energy bills, travel tickets and all of their purchases for the year. In return they got a figure, telling them their carbon footprint for the previous three months. They would then be asked to pay a levy based on this figure – which rose to a punitive level if a threshold was crossed.

Geavis spurned the carbon assessors and always liked to fill in the return himself; it gave him a sense of pride to master the bureaucratic language.

But it was also a little perilous to do the work. Make a mistake and he could face a swingeing fine.

No-one could get away with falsifying the information. Until a few years previously, it had been possible to conceal expenditure – no-one could prove, say, that you had bought a wild bean pizza on a particular date. But that had all gone when banknotes and coins were abolished. The only way to buy things now was via a card or mobile phone. Every transaction was transmitted to a database for the Executive for Personal Carbon budgeting – or was rumoured to be.

What was the code for the banana cake he had bought on 27 January? And how many carbon points had it had? Was it 300 or 500 grams? He asked Olivia, but she hadn't a clue – she couldn't find the code, either. It mattered, because from his calculations he would come out pretty close to the annual carbon limit for a grade 32 private citizen – a privileged white male between the ages of 65 and 70.

"It's going to come out too high," he said, plunging his head into his hands. "That'll be an extra £1,000. It'll mean no trip to Clacton next year."

"But do we enjoy Clacton that much anyway?" said Olivia. "It's not the same as it was in the old days, when there were lights and music on the seafront. I could quite happily stay at home."

Geavis' work was interrupted by the arrival at the door of a girl called Bunty. He recognised her as the daughter of a couple from several doors down, and assumed that she was still at school. She was. But recently she had also been appointed a climate influencer, and as part of the arrangement she was expected to call on neighbours and advise them on how to make changes to their lifestyle for the good of the planet.

Geavis resented the idea of being told what to do by someone so youthful, but she was so full of smiles and persuasion that he allowed her into the house anyway.

"Mr Geavis, I'm just dying to run through with you a few things about our action plan for extreme weather," she began. "As you probably know, events like the big storm are going to be happening more and more – unless we take action, right now."

It became immediately clear to Geavis that Bunty was reciting from a prepared script, and he wanted to tell her so, but couldn't quite bring himself to. Would it not sound a bit rude to say that to a 17-year-old girl? Besides, it was a script so carefully put together, so tightly delivered, that it allowed him no chance to interrupt.

"We've really got to get those greenhouse emissions right down – immediately. And sadly, it's not something we can do without taking a close look at our lifestyles. Shall we have a look at yours? And remember, it's your children's futures that depend on the decisions that you make today."

With hardly a blink she was looking around. "Let's have a look at how you are heating your home" He got a tick for that – he showed her his air source heat pump and she said, "Wow, that's given me a good feeling. You're making inroads on that carbon footprint of yours."

Geavis couldn't seem to stop himself showing her round the house, letting her inspect everything. Was it because it gave him a sense of warm satisfaction every time she signalled her approval? She smiled and gave him the thumbs up at his solar panels, insisted on high-fiving him when she saw his triple glazing – though the gesture didn't come naturally to him and he offered only a limp palm. Before he knew it, he was showing her the contents of his fridge.

At this point, Bunty's tone began to change. There was nothing wrong with the celery, the swedes, the parsnips – they all passed muster. But then she spotted a pair of guavas which Olivia had brought home from the market the previous Tuesday.

Bunty picked one up and waved it at him, her expression changing to a grimace. "That's given me a sad face, Mr Geavis. Have you thought of the food miles in this?" Geavis shook his head. "Come on," she continued, "that's tropical. We don't need to appropriate other cultures' diets – and push up our emissions in the process."

"It was just a treat," said Geavis, feebly.

"Last year, 3,500 people died in tropical storms, and it's all our fault."

Geavis stood and looked at her, blankly. Bunty was beginning to irritate him now, but he couldn't think of a way to extract himself from the situation.

"It's quite a big fridge, too," said Bunty. "How many of you live here? Two? A fridge half the size would do you. And remember, if

31

you base your diet around seasonal local vegetables, you won't need to refrigerate them."

Geavis decided to let Bunty finish surveying his house to her satisfaction, and he tried his best to nod at whatever she said, while he thought of something different entirely. But he couldn't help asking her, when she had reached his second bathroom and berated him for possessing a power shower: "How did you become a climate influencer?"

"I did a school project," she said. "I found out all the ways my teacher was wasting energy. Then, I had to go on three marches and interview three people on the street and tell them they were selfish."

"Was that it?"

"What more did you want me to do? Those are pretty big things."

"And what do you hope to get out of it?"

"I want to do enough assessments to win a trip to Florida."

"To Florida? How come?"

"All the things I'm telling you to do save carbon emissions... I can tot them up in the app and it will tell me how much carbon I've offset. If it's enough, I can fly to next year's climate conference. It's such fun, according to people who have been."

"Are you supposed to be telling me this?"

"Why not? I'm proud of saving so much carbon."

"But what if I don't take your advice?"

Bunty looked puzzled at this. "But why wouldn't you? Surely you want to stop climate change, don't you? We've just seen how it's killing people."

Geavis said nothing, and Bunty left a few moments afterwards, feeling sufficiently disturbed by his offhand manner that she later felt the need to share her experience with her contacts on the social media site, Mob. Her confidence had been deflated by what she saw as Geavis' unexpectedly negative attitude, and she took the next day off school to recover.

As for Geavis, he thought he had concealed his anger from her. But as soon as she was out of the house, he started muttering to himself. How had a 17-year-old girl been able to become a climate influencer, when he had not? Did his 30 years' experience in meteorology count for nothing?

It was a year since he had himself applied for the honour. To bolster his case, he submitted to the climate influencer interview board the hand-written weather records he had meticulously kept for the past 40 years, taken from the miniature weather stations in his back garden. He also kept records of his roses: which day of the year the buds had appeared and when they had flowered. He thought it a valuable record, because it combined meteorological and horticultural data, and he knew of no-one who had kept such a combination of records anywhere in the Thames Estuary area. Surely that would be of great use to science?

He had memorised his data, so that when it came to his interview he could recite it. In the first decade, he said, the mean daily maximum temperature had been 13.5 Celsius. In the second decade it had leapt to 14.6 Celsius, and in the third decade to 15.0 Celsius. But it had fallen back slightly in the fourth decade, to 14.9 Celsius. "It surprised me," he said, "but it goes to show how much noise there is in climate data. Decade on decade, the weather in one place can be quite variable."

He thought he explained it well, but he detected a drop in metaphorical temperature among the seven on the interview panel. The warm welcome he had been given a few moments earlier descended into cold glares. After a brief silence, a man with plaited hair who had been introduced simply as 'Firkin', and who was slouching on his seat so that his battered boots with missing laces protruded from beneath the table, asked incredulously: "Are you really trying to tell us that your garden is cooling down? The only place in the world?"

"It can't be right," said a woman with a ring through her nose. "You might consider adjusting some of your data in line with established fact."

The suggestion seemed so alien to Geavis that at first he didn't know how to respond. Eventually he said: "But that is what the thermometer is saying! I can't fiddle with the figures just because I think they ought to say something different."

"Maybe your roses are shading the thermometer," said Firkin. "It's got to be something like that. The Earth's literally on fire; it ain't getting cooler. "

"It's not permissible to publish data which is not in line with established science," said the woman with the nose ring. "It needs to be harmonised with the models."

"But my temperature records *are* the science!" said Geavis.

It cut no ice, and he had to allow the conversation to move on. A fresh-faced girl who could not have been more than 20, and who had managed to keep smiling when her co-panellists had not, was the next to speak.

"If you could ban one thing to save the climate from breakdown, what would it be?"

Geavis was lost; he hadn't anticipated the question. "Must I ban anything?" he said. He then watched as the panel members exchanged outraged glances.

"We're not going to get anywhere without banning things, are we?" Firkin said.

That had pretty much been that, aside from Geavis having to fill in the privilege form – a form everyone had to complete whenever they met state officialdom. He had filled in these forms so frequently it had become second nature. Often, he felt tempted to lie and put himself down as something he knew he was not – something that would push his privilege score as low as he could reasonably get it. Would anyone catch him out if he said that he was part Inuit, or from one of the other peoples who had been classified as climatically oppressed? He thought it unlikely, but still he couldn't quite bring himself to write down a false answer.

The verdict from the climate influencer interview board came as no surprise. "We are not convinced that you would have anything to offer that would justify your being appointed to this position," it read. "But we wish you the best with your weather records and hope that they will contribute to your education on the climate emergency."

He read no further, discarding the letter before, he hoped, he had had chance to absorb it and allow it to upset him. But still the sense of rejection ate away at him, even 12 months on.

*

In the days after Bunty's visit, Geavis noticed coverage of the Guy Fawkes Night storm starting to take a subtle turn. Until now, the public mood had seemed focussed on two questions: why hadn't the storm been forecast, and why hadn't the Thames Barrier been closed? A group representing the Deptford victims pressed mercilessly on these issues.

"Why didn't the warnings reach us?" Evie Wilks, spokesperson for the Deptford victims' group, asked at a public meeting. "The warnings got to the people in the flats above us – and the floodwaters were never going to reach them, anyway. It's like we were thrown into the waters to fend for ourselves while rich people kept their feet dry. So tell us the truth: why were we left to drown?"

The government could give no answers, beyond saying that the public inquiry would look into such issues and it would be better if they didn't comment beforehand. The prime minister, Sheila Gregory, tried to hold this line when she visited the scene of the Deptford deaths.

"Please forgive me if I cannot provide answers today," she tried to tell a raucous and pulsating crowd. "I know some of you will find that unsatisfactory, but really, it would be unacceptable for me, or anyone else, to try to make judgements on this before we have the proper evidence before us."

The crowd was not impressed. Gregory had to retreat quickly into her car, which sped away – a window being cracked by a projectile as it did so. To add to the ugliness of the scene, a protester's leg was broken, and the incident formed the basis of angry exchanges for days afterwards, prompting a tearful Gregory several times to retreat to her private quarters in Downing Street and contemplate resignation.

While anger at the government rumbled on, the media simultaneously began to press the weather forecasters as well. Newspaper reports began to confirm what Geavis already knew: that the predicted path of the storm had been wrong. At around 6.00 pm it had swung unexpectedly southwards. The head of the Agency for Modelling Climate Chaos, Guy Hovis – whom Geavis knew slightly from his days in the profession – agreed to be interviewed about this on breakfast television.

"We have to hold our hands up and say we got it wrong," Hovis said. "But it is a fact that with climate change, storms are becoming more unpredictable. They are developing in ways our models sometimes struggle to cope with. It is simply not possible to give forecasts with any confidence, now.

The climate emergency is making our computers and network of recording stations redundant. We need more investment."

"That's a cop out," Geavis told Olivia. "If I could see the storm turn while sitting up in my office and watching a satellite image, why couldn't he?"

"Maybe they did see it and they just didn't believe it," said Olivia. It was a remark she intended as comforting, but which provided no solace for her husband.

Hovis' interview succeeded in deflecting much of the anger aimed at his organisation. He was surprised at how readily the normally combative interviewer, Suza Shamon, accepted his explanation. "So, you're saying that we can't predict the weather anymore?" she asked.

"Yes," replied Hovis. "Not only are we going to face more severe storms, but we are also going to have to face up to the fact they will sometimes turn up on our doorstep unannounced."

"Sounds terrifying," said Shamon, enjoying a fleeting sense of pride that she had extracted a scoop from a scientist, only later regretting that she had not felt qualified to challenge his assertion.

Sarah Downwood noted, too, how easily Shamon had accepted Hovis' explanation and quickly moved to take advantage of the situation. Within an hour she was making a statement on the steps of her ministry building.

"We have just heard it from the head of the Agency for Modelling Climate Chaos that the weather is becoming less and less predictable," she said. "That's just one more of the effects of climate change that we are having to cope with. If I sound alarmist, I make no apologies for that, because sooner or later we have to face up to the reality of the crisis we are in."

Her advisers, eager not to let the opportunity pass, began to shift the emphasis of the promised public inquiry. Where previously it was to be focussed on the delayed flood warning and on the response of emergency services, now it would have a wider – though she hoped also shallower – remit. It would look the new threat of ever more unpredictable storms, and propose even more severe measures for cutting back greenhouse gas emissions.

As if to underline the point, Downwood called reporters back in the late afternoon to make a further announcement.

"We have decided that as from today, the Ministry for the Climate

Emergency will be renamed, to reflect the situation that we are in, more accurately. From now on it will be the Ministry for the Climate Crisis."

*

Aside from Geavis himself, at least one person was not happy with the Agency for Modelling Climate Chaos' explanation for why the storm had not been forecast. A producer on Radio South Essex remembered how, on Guy Fawkes Night, someone claiming to be a retired meteorologist had rung up giving prior warning of the storm, about four hours before the station's own weather forecaster drew attention to it. At the time, the producer hadn't taken the caller very seriously, but after hearing Guy Hovis on the national news, he had an idea.

Why not call the retired meteorologist and have him on the programme to comment?

It took quite an effort, of rifling through old notebooks to find the meteorologist's telephone number, alongside a scribbled name he couldn't quite read. The producer rang the number and Geavis answered.

"Hi, is that Mr Gears?" asked the producer.

"Geavis."

"Ah, sorry. It's Radio South Essex. You remember that you rang in on Guy Fawkes night to tell us you spotted the storm? In light of what the head of the Agency for Modelling Climate Chaos has said today, we'd like you back on the show."

Geavis agreed immediately, but Olivia could not see why he would want to go on the show – and told him so.

"What is there to be gained? But there's an awful lot to lose. It's a highly emotive subject."

But Geavis saw no harm in it. "It's my responsibility to share what professional knowledge I have. Perhaps my input might help improve forecasts for another time."

A couple of hours later he was sitting in the studio, rigid as he watched lights come on and off, and astonished by how relaxed the presenter was as he waited for the 'on air' light.

"Ten days ago, as you cannot have forgotten, South Essex was struck by one of the fiercest storms in living memory," the presenter began. "What you might not remember is that a few hours before the storm hit, we broadcast this weather forecast."

Then he played back a clip about how an unnamed listener had called in, to warn of the approaching storm.

"I'm pleased that we passed on his warning, but perhaps we didn't take him seriously enough. As you know, the storm turned out to be far stronger, far more dangerous than the forecasts we had been receiving from the Agency for Modelling Climate Chaos that evening. It turns out that the listener in question was himself a retired meteorologist called Bryan Geavis, who lives in Campton-on-Sea. And he's with me in the studio right now. Bryan, take us through it. How did you know a storm was coming and we didn't?"

"It's really rather simple," said Geavis. "I subscribe to a website that provides live satellite images, and it became clear to me at around 5.00 pm that the storm was not taking the path the weather forecasts had predicted – it was turning southwards, straight towards us."

"And why do you think most forecasters missed that? Surely they were looking at the same satellite images as you were?"

"I don't know. You'll have to ask them. But it is clear there is something wrong with their forecasting models."

"We heard yesterday the minister for the climate emergency – sorry, the climate *crisis*, we now have to get used to saying – that storms are becoming less predictable. Is that true?"

"But I could see it six hours ahead, so I don't think that excuse stands up at all. When I saw the storm I personally went down to the seafront to warn as many people as I could. Had others spotted the correct passage of the storm, then I am sure lives could have been saved. "

Geavis left the studio a few moments later, feeling pleased with himself. He had said his bit and he had been listened to. It felt as if a weight had been lifted from his shoulders. Maybe his intervention would achieve something; in future the forecasters would adjust their forecasting models – or at least look more carefully at the satellite images as they came in.

A few hours later he was surprised to receive another call, this time from

Diversity TV in London – the organisation formerly known as the BBC. Word had spread of his interview on South Essex Radio, and Suza Shamon wanted to interview him on her own show in the morning – this time to a national audience, and on television too.

Geavis was minded to seize the chance to tell the whole story. But Olivia, again, was less keen. "You'll be a damned fool to do it," she scolded. "What, after the prime minister's car was set upon in Deptford?"

"But I can't just let it go," said Geavis. "The Met Office was wrong, and now it is making things worse. There are times when you have to stick your head above the parapet, you know, even when there are bullets flying around."

"I know what's going to happen. They'll get someone else on the show to hack you to pieces."

But Geavis couldn't see what she meant. He was surprised to have enjoyed his time in the local radio studio, felt it had been profitable and now was his chance, nay his *duty*, to put his case to the entire nation.

*

The Suza Shamon Show was an early morning programme, meaning that he had to take the first train to London. There was no time for breakfast, but if his journey went well there would be time to catch something to eat before he went into the studio.

As it turned out, the train was 20 minutes late – repair work following the storm was blamed – and Geavis felt a little flustered as he made his way up from Oxford Circus. Nevertheless, there were still a few minutes for him to visit a coffee shop and buy what he had set his heart upon: a roll filled with crispy 'rasher' – a product which, he had to admit, almost tasted like real bacon.

But there was a problem when he tried to pay. His card was refused, and it took a member of staff to come across and explain why: the shop did not have it on record that he had signed the social pledge. Thus, his payment would not be accepted.

The social pledge was a list of 20 or so questions, all of which had to be answered in the affirmative. Most shops and restaurants had started to use it – persuaded to do so by activist groups who threatened to boycott their stores if they did not make their customers sign.

"Look, I'm in a hurry," said Geavis. "Can't I leave it out this time? I'll sign it next time."

The member of staff shook his head. "Sorry, sir. No pledge, no breakfast."

Geavis reluctantly got out his phone, downloaded the coffee shop's app and started to scroll through the questions. Yet, in spite of being short of time, he refused to do what most people did: quickly tick all the boxes without reading the questions. He already knew, roughly, what the questions in the social pledge were because he had filled it in for other shops, but still it didn't feel right to him to sign something without reading it thoroughly.

"I accept the reality of the climate crisis and recognise that the dangers from it will only get worse," read the first question. Snarling, he clicked on the 'yes' box.

"I recognise inequality in all its forms and accept the collective guilt of all people of my privilege." He ticked again, but hissed under his breath: what has this got to do with having a breakfast roll? "Respecting the equal rights of animals, I will not eat or use animal product." He ticked, but started to ask himself how much he really wanted this roll, or whether he had time to go and find one of the diminishing number of cafes which had yet to adopt the social pledge. "I accept the rights of women to make their own decisions over their reproductive health."

That was enough. He looked at his watch and realised there were now only 10 minutes before he was due in the television studio. If he carried on there would be no time to eat the roll anyway. He left, muttering "This is ridiculous!" to no-one in particular and ran up the street, his tummy rumbling.

He arrived at the studio to be handed a pass – and a piece of paper carrying an identical set of questions to those he had just been answering. "It's the social pledge," the receptionist told him. "Everyone has to sign it now before they can go on air."

"Why?"

"It's for everyone's safety."

"Safety? What do you mean?"

"We're told to say that only approved opinions are welcome on Diversity TV."

Geavis hesitated. The receptionist continued. "They've phoned down to say they need you up there now, so they can mic you up. So you really need to fill this in now."

Geavis snarled but said nothing. This time, he didn't even stop to ask the questions; he just ticked them all so as to be done with it. Maybe the people who were in the habit of blindly ticking all the questions were right. The social pledge was meaningless, he told himself, so what did it matter?

There was no time for the make-up artist to apply powder to Geavis' red and puffy face, so he was led straight into the studio and sat down beneath a studio light which exacerbated his sweating. People who saw the programme later told him he looked ill, but he had no inkling of his appearance as a producer counted down and cameras began to move in from all directions.

Geavis had a clear view of Suza Shamon, whom he thought looked strangely waxy in the flesh. He hardly noticed the bearded young man sitting next to him on the sofa before Suza introduced them both.

"Earlier in the week, if you remember, we had the head of the Agency for Modelling Climate Chaos on the programme, telling us that weather forecasters didn't predict the fatal storm on Guy Fawkes Night because the weather is becoming less predictable due to climate change," she began. "We all rely on weather forecasts, but if climate change is going to make it impossible to predict the weather, what does it mean for us all? I have with me today Bryan Geavis, who is an amateur meteorologist, and Dr Aric Reissner, who is an expert in weather patterns in the Canadian Arctic. Bryan, we've asked you on today because you say you *did* know the storm was coming. How come you knew and the experts didn't?"

Geavis was offended by the word 'amateur'. Suza must know, surely, that he had been a professional meteorologist? He wanted to make this point, but hesitated just a moment too long, and before he could say anything Suza followed up with: "Was it tea leaves, or just a hunch?"

"Not tea leaves, of course not," he said. "I was watching the satellite images of the storm and I saw it turn. It suddenly changed path, so instead

41

of drifting eastwards towards the Northumbrian coast it suddenly dived southwards, towards the Thames Estuary. I don't know why they didn't see that at the Agency for Modelling Climate Chaos. I don't know what the delay was."

"But they've got it right today," said Suza. "They said it would be murky and cold, and that's exactly what it was when I came in. But turning to you, Dr Reissner, is it true that these big storms are becoming less predictable?"

"Very much so," said Reissner. "I've been working with the Inuit people, understanding how they forecast the weather. And they say that 40 years ago they used to be able to set off on a hunt lasting several days, confident that the weather would hold. Now, that's very important for them, because they need the weather to stay cold so they don't fall through the ice. But in recent years they tell me they can't do it anymore. They can't trust the ice because the cold periods last less long – they just don't know when the weather is going to change. That is having a very big impact on their lives and is one of the many ways in which climate change is devastating societies, both human and animal."

All the while, Geavis noted, Suza was nodding. "That sounds pretty tough for them," she said. "More storms, stronger storms and less predictable storms. That's a terrible triple whammy. And all because of climate change?"

"Absolutely," said Reissner. "One hundred percent."

"So that sounds pretty unarguable, Bryan," said Suza. "And when you've got the experts telling you that, you wonder what the debate is."

"I can only say what I saw with my own eyes," said Geavis. "And I saw that storm turn at least three hours before the Agency for Modelling Climate Chaos told us that it was heading straight for us. Had they seen it earlier, then I am sure that lives could have been saved."

"So, you're questioning the professional meteorologists, the scientists who make the forecasts? Really?"

"I know the science behind storms. I have been watching them for four decades. I can read a synoptic chart. I presume the people at the Agency for Modelling Climate Chaos can, too. But that night they got it wrong, and fatally so."

"Dr Reissner, do you find this credible?"

"I wasn't here on the night the storm broke and I wasn't watching, I'm afraid. I was up on Hudson's Bay observing the very stark changes in the climate up there. I flew several thousand miles and saw no snow and ice – and that's a record this time of year. If we don't keep our eyes open to what's happening, we're doomed. Hotter temperatures; rising seas; wilder, less predictable weather. Everyone should know that. Frankly, I'm surprised even that we're still having this kind of conversation."

"The conversation I am trying to have is about last week's storm," said Geavis, getting a little flustered, "not about the climate in Hudson's Bay."

"But we've got to join the dots and see how it is all linked," said Dr Reissner. "Lack of ice in Hudson's Bay, storm which appears out of nowhere in England. It's all connected, and we've got to start accepting that pretty damned quick. We know what we're heading for otherwise: an uninhabitable Earth."

"This is what I find so absurd," said Geavis. "You speak with such great certainty about what is going to happen in decades' time, but then you swallow the Agency for Modelling Climate Chaos' claim that they can't see a storm coming hours ahead."

"You think we don't know what's up with the climate?"

"That's not the point I was making."

"Well, come on, tell us. Are you questioning that we are headed for climate collapse?"

"I don't know. It's not what concerns me. What I *am* trying to say is that we have the head of the Agency for Modelling Climate Chaos saying he didn't see a storm coming. Well, I saw it coming."

"The luck of the amateur, perhaps?" said Suza.

"I'm not an amateur. I was a professional meteorologist for 30 years."

"Professional? Who did you work for?"

Geavis had not anticipated this question, and it caught him cold. What was he to say? No-one dared admit to having worked for an oil company, not anymore. Except for a small number of licensed suppliers – who imported the fuel required to keep planes in the air for the benefit of climate influencers, and a few other such uses – the oil industry had been wound up years before. Its once-great corporations had been felled by lawsuits, which had sucked them dry. Their wealth had been redistributed to communities around the world claiming reparations for climate change.

Lawyers acting for the victims hadn't stopped at the corporations themselves. Anyone who had held a senior position at an oil company was considered fair game. Most oil executives had not waited around: they had disappeared, changed their names and started new lives in South America, Sub-Saharan Africa, the Gulf, who knew where? There were said to be communities of them living it up somewhere in the Amazon – although these had proved elusive. Occasionally, a former executive would be sighted, or someone would have claimed to have identified them. A hunt would begin, with the intention of civil lawsuits and criminal prosecution to follow. But so far, few had been caught.

Geavis believed himself to have been a small cog at Albion Oil, too small for anyone to be bothered with. Indeed, the divers and the oil rig workers were often spoken of as victims of the evil industry within which they had once worked. Even so, he didn't feel confident to admit to his former employment. He wavered, leaving an agonising pause that ended up being terminated by Suza:

"Well, thank you to Bryan Geavis, a sometime meteorologist who can't remember where he worked and to Dr Aric Reissner, an expert on climate change in the Arctic. I'll be watching those weather forecasts with interest. And now, a woman who has cut her carbon emissions by travelling everywhere on a unicycle…"

Geavis was ushered from the sofa, had his microphone removed and was escorted to the main entrance, where he walked out into a descending fog. He had a sense that his interview had gone wrong, but he couldn't tell why. Had Suza had it in for him? He felt she had. But why? And why had the Canadian man been invited? He hadn't been asked the right questions, he hadn't been talking about the same thing.

The more Geavis mulled the interview over, the more it bothered him. By the time he got back to Oxford Circus tube station he found himself looking up the academic on his phone. Reinhold, was it? No, Reissner. And Eric? No, here he was: Dr Aric Reissner – an anthropologist, it said.

Anthropologist? So why had he been passed off as if he were a climate scientist? It was outrageous.

It carried on bothering him most of the way home, but by the time his train was passing through London's outer suburbs his mind turned to other things. How awful these winter fogs had become. Summer days were often now beautifully clear, compared with those in the days of petrol and diesel vehicles; everyone who could remember that time remarked on the clarity of the air. But winter was another matter. Smog had become commonplace – a result, many believed, of bungled efforts to reduce carbon emissions. Buildings had been insulated and hermetically sealed so that, in theory, they would need very little heating. Then the gas grid had been turned off in the belief that fossil fuels would no longer be required to heat homes.

But soon afterwards, the ineffectiveness of the insulation work had become apparent. Cowboy builders, paid to do hundreds of houses at a time, had cut corners and then run off with the money. Heat continued to drain out through walls, yet now it was much harder to replace. Efforts to seal buildings had left them with inadequate ventilation, so that many houses became damp and riddled with mould and mildew. The electricity grid could not cope with the much greater demands than had been anticipated, with the result that power cuts frequently had to be scheduled, street by street.

Deprived of their gas boilers, people took to lighting open fires instead, burning whatever came to hand. Logs if they could procure and afford them, general rubbish if they could not. On windy days, the foul fumes quickly dispersed, but on still days thousands of belching chimneys promoted a Stygian gloom.

It was not strictly permissible to light open fires, and at first offenders had been caught and fined. But what could the authorities do? People were cold.

A baby in Wanstead, her cot pressed up against a damp wall, had died of pneumonia and the tone of the debate changed. A humbled Sarah Downwood, who had previously encouraged a crackdown against polluters, was forced to climb down.

"It has become clear that some of the insulation work at the heart of our climate emergency plan has proved ineffective," she told parliament. "Through no fault of their own, many householders have found themselves

45

unable to keep their homes warm, in one case with tragic results. Therefore, while the ineffectiveness of the insulation programme is investigated and put right, I am announcing today that open fires will be tolerated for a limited period."

But the investigation dragged on and came up with few solutions, and the 'limited period' had been stretched ever further.

While Geavis was getting off the train, the murk rekindled an idea in his head. It was something he had discussed with Olivia a number of times: the thought of emigrating to join their daughter, Tamsin, in Brazil. Maybe people would say it was a case of the grass being greener on the other side, but the more they read her messages, the more it seemed to Geavis that life was better there. Tamsin had spoken of barbecues – of fish, beef and all the things Geavis missed. It sounded easier to travel, even to fly – and without having to be appointed as a climate influencer. Had the Brazilian government been less stringent at applying the rules, which had been agreed by almost the entire world to tackle the climate emergency? Geavis didn't know, but he had heard plenty of rumours that was the case.

So far, inertia had won, and Geavis and Olivia had not been able to pull themselves away from the place they knew. But how much would it take, he wondered as he let himself back into his house, before they were moved to put their half-formed plan into action?

He didn't intend to bring up the subject as soon as he got home, but he found Olivia heaped on a sofa beneath a duvet, shivering.

"Did you see the interview?" he asked her.

"I couldn't. They cut off the electricity again. It's our turn, apparently. They could at least have told us."

"No wind, no sun – I should have guessed. There's not enough power in the grid."

Geavis eased himself beneath the duvet and they both thought, silently, of how things used to be; back when they never gave a thought to electricity, water or anything like that; when they could jump in the car and go wherever they wanted; when they used to fly off on foreign holidays. At first, they dared not exchange these thoughts, so conditioned had they become to the idea that the old ways of life were a crime against the environment.

It had become risky to admit that you missed what had become known as 'the selfish times'. You held back your private, guilty memories. Express them publicly and you knew you would face a dressing-down. You knew that children would shout at you, and even close friends might glower. So you kept quiet, and consigned them to a fantasy land, to be visited from time to time, only when alone.

But underneath the duvet, in the half hour before the lights came back on and the house began to warm up again, Geavis and Olivia did not hold themselves back. "Remember Istanbul? Remember Goa?" They exchanged stories and felt tears welling up as they said things they would never have said elsewhere. "Everything is all so glum now. It is so without colour." And they began to plot. Would it be possible for them to reach Brazil and set up afresh there? Were they still young enough to pull it off?

One thing was for sure: if they were going to realise their dream, the sooner they went about it, the better.

3

Amber had not quite reached the age at which she would feel shy conversing with her friends on social media while in the same room as her parents. Nor was she consciously aware of the dilemma her parents felt about allowing her to use her phone without supervision. Would they know – would *she* know – if she were falling victim to a bully? What if one of those friends was not who they claimed to be? There were stories too horrible to contemplate, yet her parents couldn't really stand over her while she contacted her friends. They settled for a kind of halfway house, where they gently encouraged her to do her online socialising in full view in the family living room, in the hope that if something were awry they would detect it in her demeanour.

Thus, she was happily sprawled on the sofa staring into her phone while her father sat reading a few feet away. As a result, he was quickly able to spot a sudden flash of puzzlement on her face.

What was wrong? Was she being sucked into something she didn't understand?

"Everything okay?" he asked.

"Daddy, why is Grandad trending?"

"Trending? What do you mean?"

"Everyone's talking about him."

Adam asked to have a look at Amber's phone and saw that she was on the fashionable social media site, Mob. Sure enough, there was a shot of his father's face, looking tired and puce. He scrolled down and read: "Disgraceful moment Suza invites shameless denier onto her sofa". He read on. "Diversity TV has to answer for this. Thought these loonies had been

48

taken off air." Another post read: "Suza's fake meteorologist needs turning over." Then he caught one which said: "What Diversity TV idiot got this w*nker on the show?"

His initial reaction was: how has that sort of filth managed to get through? He had tried so hard to set the parental controls on his daughter's phone, yet now he felt fooled. If the controls had been confounded by a mere asterisk, what else had she been reading?

But before he could think further along these lines it sank in that it was his own father being talked about. Suza? She was the woman who had the TV breakfast show, surely. What had his father been doing on the programme and what on earth had he said?

Adam walked to the other side of the room, away from Amber, taking her phone with him as he played a short clip of film of Geavis' interview. He wasn't much the wiser after seeing it, establishing only that his father seemed to be saying he didn't know if the world was heading for climate collapse and he wasn't terribly concerned about it.

Adam knew that these weren't wise things to say. What was the context, though? He read more and more posts, which seemed to get ever ruder, and still he couldn't work it out.

Did his father know he was being talked about in this way? Adam called him to find out. Yes, Geavis did know, although he had only just picked up on it, thanks to a phone call from a friend. "I knew it hadn't gone well," said Geavis. "But why are they picking on me like that? Surely it is the Agency for Modelling Climate Chaos they should be cross with? Didn't they understand my point?"

Geavis at first resolved not to read the comments that were being made about him, yet quickly curiosity overtook him and he found himself drawn to his computer. Many of the comments were worse, far worse, than he had imagined. He sensed hatred. Maybe individually the comments didn't read so badly, but it was the sheer volume of material that unnerved him. It was as if people were whipping each other into a rage – and over something that seemed to him so trivial: his comment that he didn't know whether the world was in climate crisis or not.

There were many levels of anger and rudeness in what he read, but everything seemed to focus on one thing: the idea that it had been wrong for Diversity TV to invite him on the show. "If morons want to deny the truth they should do it in silence," read one comment. What struck Geavis was that only a week earlier, everyone had seemed to be in agreement – that the Agency for Modelling Climate Chaos had got it wrong, that they had failed to forecast the storm, and with fatal consequences. All this seemed to have been forgotten by the people who were posting these remarks; they seemed universally to be taking the agency's side. He couldn't account for why attitudes had changed so quickly.

He asked himself why he had weakened, why he had bothered to log onto Mob and read this stuff when he had resolved not to. "It'll pass," he told himself. "Better keep my head down for a couple of days."

He was just about to shut down his computer, go away and do something else when he caught a comment that froze him.

"Prosecute him," it read, directing the police to a short video clip from the show. "You've got all you need."

Geavis was well aware that he could be accused of breaking the social pledge he had signed before appearing on the television. He had ticked a box acknowledging that the climate crisis 'would only get worse' – but had taken a different line during the interview. But the social pledge had no legal force. Breaking it might cause him problems when shopping or visiting a restaurant, but it certainly wouldn't land him in jail.

The bigger problem was whether his comments could be construed as climate change denial – something which *was* now a criminal offence. Prosecutions were rare, yet from time to time the authorities felt the need to make an example of someone. Tyra Gaunt, now writing for a small-circulation magazine, *The Controversialist*, had herself fallen foul of the law over an article questioning whether human activities had had anything to do with rising temperatures – if indeed temperatures were increasing at all. "And if they *are* rising then that's just fine by me. If I can get a tan on Bognor beach rather than having to schlep myself down to the Med, then bring it on, I say!"

There was little doubt that she had broken the law. But what would it achieve, some asked, throwing her into prison – other than to make a martyr of her? There were worries, too, that an overly severe sentence could provoke a human rights challenge on the grounds of freedom of expression.

"Nonsense," argued opposition leader Jake Raglan. "Freedom of expression doesn't allow you to shout 'fire!' in a crowded theatre – and neither does it allow you to shout 'there's no fire' when the Earth really is on fire."

Shortly afterwards, the prime minister, Sheila Gregory, was caught on the spot in a TV interview and asked whether she thought Gaunt should be prosecuted. She tried to avoid giving a direct answer, figuring that it was a question for the courts, not her, and that in any case she hadn't read the offending article.

"We've all got to take responsibility on this, er, most critical of issues," she said. But it was not enough. She was pressed over and over, until she was asked: "What are you going to do about the hard right elements who are pushing this sinister agenda?"

She sighed and said: "From what I have heard, these were totally unacceptable comments to write and, yes, where people have broken the law they should be made to answer for that."

Crown prosecutors had taken it as a signal to move in. Reluctant magistrates thought it unwise to send Gaunt to jail and settled instead for handing the editor a large fine and forcing closure of his magazine.

The prosecution set a precedent, and there had been a small trickle of cases in recent days. A teacher had been suspended and fined after telling his pupils, "Don't worry, kids, it's all a hoax" – though he insisted he had only been joking. A man in Shropshire was bound over for standing up at a council meeting and shouting: "Bollocks to green taxes. They're killing my business and what for? No reason at all – just so a lucky few can make money out of us!"

But still no-one had been sent to jail – not even an evangelical priest who claimed that rising temperatures were nothing to do with carbon emissions but were instead divine punishment for a society deluged in gluttony and sodomy. There was outrage when a judge had decided to fine, rather than incarcerate, him, and steadily pressure was building for someone to be made an example of.

The more Geavis thought about it, the more he comforted himself that his remarks could not possibly be construed as breaking the law on denial. Surely people would understand that he had merely been trying to say that long-term climate change was not the issue at stake – rather it was how weather forecasters had failed to foresee a storm a few hours before it had struck the country. Yet he was still bothered, and he endured three nights of broken sleep before he admitted to Olivia what had been keeping him awake.

"Of course you haven't broken the law," she said. "Just try to ignore these people who don't have anything better to do than to scroll through social media all day. The police have got better things to do."

Then she fell asleep. But he couldn't.

*

Neither Geavis nor Olivia were aware of the hours of meetings which had taken place at Diversity TV following Geavis' appearance on *The Suza Shamon Show*. Shamon's producer had been asked to account for his choice of guest. The matter went up and down the chain of command, escalating as more and more online comments were made demanding that Diversity TV be made to pay the price. But then, having risen to a crescendo, the online storm began to die down, the trolls having moved on to other things.

Public debate was beginning to focus instead on the stubborn fog, which had settled over London in the past few days. Temperatures were falling – failing to rise above freezing point even in the daytime – and the air was getting quite foul. Meanwhile, the lack of sun and wind continued to keep power generation levels too low to meet demand, and battery installations were running out of charge. There was a surge in hospital admissions thanks to an outbreak of bronchitis. Having tolerated open fires for weeks, the authorities were forced to act as pollution levels breached official limits.

"From Friday," announced Sarah Downwood in parliament, "it will no longer be permissible to light an open fire anywhere in London. Full enforcement will be in operation. This is a temporary measure until the weather clears. Now, I appreciate that it means some people will be unable to keep their homes warm, especially during the necessary blackout periods. For the benefit of anyone who feels uncomfortable or worried about their health as a result, we will be opening a series of emergency centres, where beds will be available."

Three nights later, a disturbance erupted at one of those centres, in a sports complex in Haringey. An embryonic protest group staged a sit-in. Their putative leader, a roofer by the name of Dave Bodger, spent the morning shouting the group's demands through a megaphone.

"For too long the poor of this city have been neglected," he said, and his words were greeted with cheers. "There's electricity for the rich. There's lights on in Mayfair. There's lights on in Chelsea. There's lights on in Hampstead! But for us? The lights have gone out. We're told by the government that prices have to rise and electricity has to be rationed to tackle global warming. What I say is: come and try sitting in one of our houses in Haringey, Hackney or the East End – and tell us then that the world is warming up. What I say is: get that power back on, now!"

In a radio phone-in, Sarah Downwood was asked what the government was going to do. Why had the power cuts not been foreseen? Were there no emergency generators that could be spirited from somewhere?

"We are assessing all options," she said, "but let me assure you of one thing. There is no truth whatsoever in the allegation that wealthy districts are being favoured over poorer ones. All London homes are on a strict rotation of outages, with no-one spared."

Refuting the rumours did her no good at all. Dave Bodger refused to believe her and repeated his claims all the louder, this time adding: "It's pretty clear there is a deep conspiracy to keep us in the dark – literally. I say again: get that power back on now, or the people aren't going to stand for it."

That evening, a fight broke out in the main hall of the sports complex, driving some of the temporary residents back to their cold homes, where they either shivered or risked prosecution by lighting fires. Some arrived home to find that looters had taken advantage of their absence.

Downwood knew it would not do. The following day she called in the power companies for an emergency meeting. Was there no way of squeezing more electricity out of the grid? Yes, she was told, there were spare generators, but they were in Spain and it would take several days, and a lot of money, to get them to Britain.

Meanwhile, the population of London became restive. Trouble spread from Haringey to other districts, and the message became stronger. Spontaneous marches and protests broke out to the slogan 'Get the Power On.'

Downwood thought she ought to go and address the crowds, to assure them that the generators were on their way, but was dissuaded by her security staff.

"We understand everyone's frustration," she told the Commons, instead. "But we have been caught out by an unprecedented spell of calm, overcast weather." She then added, feeling just a little worried that she had not checked it with her advisers, "But this is what is so dangerous about climate change – the weather is becoming more extreme in every way. Higher temperatures, lower temperatures, stronger storms and longer periods of calm weather, too. Floods a fortnight ago and now an intense fog. That is weather-weirding and shows just how we must redouble our efforts to get those carbon emissions down to zero."

She returned to her ministerial office a little concerned: was it okay, she asked her advisers, if she blamed the fog on climate change? It wasn't strictly true, they told her; what evidence they had from the eastern Pacific was that fog was declining as temperatures rose. But they told her not to worry. Nobody questioned this sort of thing anymore, for fear of falling foul of the law on climate change denial.

The advisers were right: there were no public objections to what she said, and Dave Bodger missed it altogether. Downwood's comments were, however, noted by Geavis.

"What's she saying?" he hissed at the television as his wife tried to calm him down. "This is a normal winter anticyclone made worse by the failure to enforce clean air legislation."

He was half minded to call the local radio station and make his point, though was later pleased that Olivia managed to talk him out of it. "Just calm down," she told him. "You are becoming obsessed – and quite insufferable."

Perhaps it wouldn't be such a good idea in the circumstances, he agreed.

Dave Bodger revelled in his success in forcing the government to ship in generators. He didn't yet know it, but he had already enjoyed his moment of maximum influence. The following day, a counter-protest began. As a Get the Power On march reached the junction at Seven Sisters, it was met by a band of Greenshirts, and an ugly stand-off ensued. It had just been revealed that the generators on their way to Britain were diesel-powered, and threatened to undermine the latest national target for cutting carbon emissions.

"No to the generators! No to climate vandalism!" the Greenshirts chanted.

Watching from her west London penthouse, actress Zoe Fluff wondered if she could be of assistance. Could she help calm the situation? She took advice and decided that yes, it was her duty to stand up as a climate influencer and explain to the crowds why they needed to bear with the efforts to cut emissions. With no acting job for a week, her agent suggested to her that it would, in any case, be a good piece of reputation management.

"I know you're cold, I know you're in darkness," Fluff told the crowds in Seven Sisters Road. "But we've got to stop changing the weather, and you're all a really big part of that. I know it's really tough without power, but if it ain't green power, it's power we've got to learn to do without. So I say, why don't we all huddle together and keep each other warm?"

Her voice trailed off beneath a cheer from the crowd behind her, and angry jeering from the crowd in front of her. As tensions rose, she had to be quickly removed from the scene, though not quickly enough. A small group of protesters surrounded her car, trying to set it alight. But however hard they tried, they couldn't. Old hands, veterans of riots long in the past, tried with lighted rags – but just how could they sustain a fire in an electric car that was carrying no flammable fuel? Frustrated, they overturned the vehicle instead, and Fluff was left to flee on foot.

Later, back in her penthouse, she opined to friends that it was the worst experience she had ever had. "How is it that I can get through to a village of subsistence farmers in Mozambique, but not to Londoners?" She was cheered to read, however, claims that the climate activists were beginning to outnumber the Get the Power On brigade. "Beginning to get the message through!" she beamed to her followers on Mob, along with the hashtags #huddleforwarmth and #huddleforlove.

The power of her Mob account became clear when, within 24 hours, she had inspired Evie Wilks and the Deptford victims' group to form a #huddleforwarmth, #huddleforlove protest camp. They made a tactical retreat from the tetchy Seven Sisters Road and occupied instead the safer, more familiar territory of Trafalgar Square. An electronic clarion call went out in the evening, and as if from nowhere, by morning a crowd of 20,000 had assembled.

Wilks herself addressed the movement. "We won't be defeated by the deniers and the fascists!" she told them. "People are dying, the world is dying, and they think only of their own comfort and convenience. The generators are instruments of extinction. No way are they going to come to London. This is a fossil fuel-free city and we are going to turn them back. Let's say it to each other now: we're going to block the ports. Those generators will not be unloaded."

Her speech made the top spot in the television news, irritating Dave Bodger as he watched it from his favourite pub up in Haringey.

"Why does she get on the news?" he blurted through his beer glass. "It's the ordinary people who suffer while once again the cameras get turned on the warm and well-fed elite."

He half-made plans to gather a crowd and go down to Trafalgar Square the following day to disrupt the camp, but he couldn't hide the fact that his protest group was losing momentum. A few of his followers did try to get down to Trafalgar Square, but got lost. Many others needed to work, including Bodger himself, whose employment had been disrupted by the lack of power over the past few days.

"Well, we've made our point," he satisfied himself the next day as he hauled rolls of roofing felt up a ladder. "We've got some generators on the way and that's what matters."

He then peeled off the existing roof to find an unexpected void. "No bloody insulation at all!" he called down to his mate. "God, the cowboys they've had working on these houses. The thieves! Out to pick the pockets of those naive bastards at the ministry for climate crisis!"

*

Over in Beckton, 10-year-old Amber was undecided: should she tell her mum that she wanted to skip school to join the protest camp in Trafalgar Square or should she just sneak off as some of her friends said they were going to do? She was tempted to do the latter, but not quite daring enough to go through with it, and so she asked her mum, Chloe, for permission to skip school.

"I admire you for wanting to go," came the answer, "but I'm not happy about it. There's been trouble at these protests. And there's plenty of other people there to make a stand, so they're not going to miss you."

The sense of independence in Amber's response shocked her mother. "It's my future, Mum. It's not your right to deny me that."

Afraid that her daughter would fall for her friends' influence and go to Trafalgar Square regardless, Chloe decided on a compromise. She would take Amber to the protest the following day, but she would only spend a couple of hours there, perhaps standing a little way back from the centre of the action, so as to be able to make a quick exit in case of trouble.

In the end, Amber wore a felt-tipped banner around her neck with the words 'It's My Future'. She complained that they were too far back and couldn't hear the speeches. She also said she was cold. She asked her mum if they could get closer. Couldn't they go over to where the protesters, realising that huddling wasn't going to be enough to keep out the freezing temperatures, had lit a large bonfire to keep themselves warm?

By the end of the afternoon she was begging her mum to buy her some thermal boots. But on returning home, though shivering, she felt a sense of achievement. She had stood up and been counted, and no-one could take that away from her.

*

Between scheduled power cuts, Bryan Geavis watched television news of the riots and the protest camp dispassionately. He wasn't aware that his granddaughter and daughter-in-law had been part of the crowds. He was more interested in the anticyclone that had left Britain cloudy and becalmed for a week now, with temperatures sinking by the day.

Whenever the power was on, he couldn't help himself turning on his computer and following the weather map. Several times, the anticyclone had shown signs of slipping away to the near continent, but then it pushed back against the Atlantic fronts, which had been trying to dislodge it. It was, he mused, a bit like the Seven Sisters riot – a battle of raw power between two forces, and no-one knew which had the greater muscle.

There was no doubt, though, how the weather battle would eventually play out, because the Atlantic fronts always won in the end. On Friday night, the decisive moment came; the isobars began to shift, slowly at first and then with gathering speed.

Late that evening, Geavis took a walk down to the seafront, just for the pleasure of experiencing the first few puffs of mild south-westerly air that he knew was going to blow the smog away. The front itself made landfall on Saturday morning, bringing a blanket of rain to Scotland and northern England, while the south of the country emerged, blinking, into sunshine and a strong breeze. The wind turbines began to turn, the solar panels to absorb what sunlight they could. The power outages ceased and many of the crowds, like the smog, dispersed – save for a couple of hundred or so of hardened protesters.

Among them was Evie Wilks, who started to formulate a plan to turn their camp into the permanent seat of an alternative government.

That morning the emergency generators arrived, in secrecy, at Tilbury docks. The location had been kept secret, but Downwood went along to be photographed with the machinery as it was unloaded – just in case the riots erupted again and she felt she needed to show that she had taken action. By now, however, the power cuts had ceased and there was no need for the extra generators.

But quite apart from that, Downwood and her advisers began to notice a shift in public opinion. They had assumed that people would praise her swift action in boosting London's back-up electricity supply, and initially that seemed to be the case. But the day that electricity was restored, a photo of an emaciated polar bear had appeared on the front of many newspapers and been shared millions of times on Mob. The poor creature, it was asserted, was a starving victim of the climate emergency. This was never proven, and the provenance of the photographs never became clear. "How do they know the bear's not just old?" Geavis asked himself.

Yet it hardly seemed to matter. To many people, the animal was a victim of human intervention in the climate, and that was that. A reporter from Diversity TV showed the photograph to passers-by on a busy London road and asked them: "What is more important to you: having constant power for your hairdryer or the lives of these creatures?" Not one had plumped for the hairdryer.

"It's just awful, isn't it?" one girl sobbed into the camera in a typical response. "What we're doing to these animals. What does hair matter compared with the lives of these wonderful animals?"

Perhaps unfortunately, as the next interviewee was invited to the microphone, the previous speaker could be seen entering a hair salon.

Downwood's advisers quietly deleted the photographs of her at Tilbury docks. As for the generators themselves, they sat idle for three weeks before being shipped back to Spain.

4

Prior to his own appearance, Geavis had never watched Suza Shamon's Sunday morning TV show. Had he done so, he wondered, would he have been less overwhelmed by the whole thing and put on a stronger performance?

Like the proverbial stable door being slammed shut, he couldn't resist watching the programme in the week following his own appearance. Balancing a plate of toast on his knees, he switched on the television just as the opening credits were beginning to roll.

Suza, looking less waxy than she had appeared in the flesh, listed the day's guests, which included secretary of state for the climate crisis, Sarah Downwood, and Evie Wilks, the leader of the Deptford victims' group.

"Another week, another side of the climate crisis. As the fog finally lifts from London and the power cuts end, we ask: what has gone wrong, and how much more are we going to have to do to avert catastrophe? But first, an apology. On the show last week we had a guest, Bryan Geavis, whom we introduced as a retired meteorologist. We now realise that we should have checked his credentials more carefully. For the safety of viewers, we assure you that in future we will make sure that this error is not repeated…"

Geavis thumped the sofa so hard that his toast jumped off the plate and landed on the carpet. How could they say that! He could have quite easily proved that he had been a professional meteorologist, if only they had asked him to. What was he to do? Should he ring Diversity TV straight away? Should he write? One thing was for sure: they had made a mistake and it would have to be corrected.

He wanted to switch off the television; it would be better for him, he thought; stop him getting too worked up. Yet he couldn't stop himself listening to the interview with Evie Wilks.

"Last week it was fog," said Suza Shamon. "But we're not going to forget the storm a fortnight ago which cost the lives of 35 people. The weather seems to get weirder and weirder. I'm delighted to have with me today Evie Wilks, who so narrowly escaped death herself in that flooded basement in Deptford. She is rapidly becoming one of the leading voices of the climate crisis. Last week, she was part of the Huddle for Love camp in Trafalgar Square, protesting against the arrival of diesel generators which had been ordered from Spain to help relieve the power cuts. Evie, we know we're in crisis, but there are Londoners who would have been very pleased to see those generators."

"This is what we're up against," said Wilks. "The selfishness of a few which leads to death and suffering of the many. It's been the story throughout history: patriarchal misuse of power to oppress the weak, to oppress women, to oppress ethnic minorities, to oppress anyone who gets in the way of the privileged elite. The only difference now is that it's diesel power rather than gunfire being used to brutalise us."

"But I'm not sure the people who were calling for the generators could be described as patriarchs," said Shamon. "A lot of them were just Londoners who were trying to keep warm and feed their families…"

"Oh yeah, they'll say that, won't they? Look, the Earth is on fire. We're being drowned by rising seas, farmland is turning into desert. Animals are being wiped out in their billions. And don't tell me that someone's convenience is more important than that…"

Shamon was happy to let Wilks talk for a bit, because she wasn't sure where to take the interview. To challenge Wilks over the generators, to make the point that many Londoners were desperate to see the electricity turned back on, seemed the obvious line to take. There had been a great deal of anger over the failure of the electricity supply, and that anger ought to be voiced. In pre-production meetings there had been talk of getting Dave Bodger onto the programme to debate live with Evie Wilks, but the producer wasn't sure it was a good idea. After all, who was Bodger? For all they knew he could turn out to be climate crisis denier, just like last week's guest. It wasn't worth the risk.

What would serve the viewer better, somebody suggested, was if Wilks was challenged over the strategy of her embryonic movement. Did she really have enough people behind her to force the government's hand and persuade it to bring forward its climate agenda? Was Wilks the future of climate protest, or would her movement fizzle out?

Yet to Shamon that did not seem right. She was determined to push her point about Londoners relying on electricity just a little further. But before she could do so, Wilks broke into a coughing fit.

"That's a nasty cough you've got there," Shamon said, proffering a glass of water.

"It's the toxic air," said Wilks. "It's choking us."

As Wilks gulped down the water, a voice came through Shamon's earpiece from the production team.

"This is great, you showing some empathy. Ask her how the disaster has affected her life."

Shamon reluctantly did as she was told, and the tears welled up in Wilks' eyes. Wilks started talking about the friends she had lost and the anger that the survivors still felt. "There was a young man whom I nearly had in my grasp. I had found some steps, I was clinging onto a bannister and I was trying to urge him to keep his head above water and cling onto me. But then he was gone. They were beautiful people, those who were taken. People are dying, and the government doesn't care."

"You speak very movingly," said Shamon. "And there's no question you have a lot of support on your side. But does the Huddle for Love movement really have the numbers required to push the government?"

"It comes down to which side of history we want to be on," said Wilks. "Do you we want to be with the destroyers, or do we want to be with those who did everything they could to stop the climate cataclysm when we still had the chance? Do we want to be on the side of the killers, or on the side of love?"

Wilks and the other leaders of Huddle for Love were later to credit her performance on *The Suza Shamon Show* for the large increase in the numbers of people making their way to Trafalgar Square the following week. In the meantime, it was the turn of Sarah Downwood to face questioning from Shamon. The toughness which Shamon had wanted to put into her interview with Wilks was instead discharged against Downwood.

"You've heard it there," Shamon said. "The Earth is dying, people are being killed, wildlife wiped out. I'm finding it hard to understand why you felt it appropriate last week to import diesel generators, which you know are adding to the climate crisis."

"We have two things to balance," said Downwood. "We have the climate crisis, as you quite properly say, but at the same time there are millions of Londoners who need energy to cook meals, to keep themselves and their families warm."

"But these are the same arguments we've had for years. And look where it's got us. The weather is getting weirder and weirder. Isn't it time to bear down on this emergency once and for all?"

"But we *are*, Suza. We've introduced carbon accounting – everyone is now limited to their own personal budget, with stiff penalties if they exceed it. We've reduced those budgets year on year. This is a very proper response to the crisis."

"Crisis? Isn't it about time we stopped using that word? This is a cataclysm. How are you going to make progress if you don't recognise that?"

"We are taking this incredibly seriously. We know that humankind's very existence is on the line. We know we've got to do better, and I assure you we will do all we can to drive down those emissions still further."

"So, the generators. Will you be sending them back?"

"Well, I can't…"

"You can't *what*? You've heard the popular uprising from Trafalgar Square this week. There's very real anger that those generators are being brought into the country. What have you got to say to Evie Wilks, who lost her friends and nearly died in a storm undeniably caused by the climate cataclysm? Those generators are just making things worse, aren't they?"

"Look, these were just a few extra generators. We all already have hundreds of back-up generators placed strategically around the country. They're what keeps the lights on when energy demand is high and supply low. The past week was just an especially lax time for power generation, and so we needed a back-up supply to the back-up. I don't see why it is such a big deal."

"What? So you mean we already have diesel generators in use in Britain?"

"Yes, plenty of them. Though we are looking at ways to phase them out over time."

"How many people know this, I wonder?"

"You tell me."

Downwood had been pushed into a corner, but felt she had handled the interview well. Her advisers thought so, too. She had stayed calm in the face of hostile questioning.

But public opinion told a different story. Asked who they found more credible, Wilks or Downwood, a large majority plumped for Wilks.

"She showed her human side," one respondent told focus group in the Midlands. "As for Downwood, it's all evasion, isn't it? She's just trying to cover her back."

*

And yet, a far bigger storm was about to break over the government. Left-leaning newspaper *The Progressive* discovered that, 15 years earlier, when she was a junior MP, the prime minister had received a donation from Albion Oil to help run her office.

"PM in Pay of Big Oil," ran the headline. "Campaign for Leadership Funded by Dirty Money. Can We Trust Her?"

Sheila Gregory's office immediately went into crisis mode. Aides knew how explosive an issue this could be. Should they try to play it down, or issue an apology?

"It was only £500 – a tiny sum compared with many other donations that came to the party at the time," Gregory told her aides. "Surely no-one could hold that against me?"

Her staff were shocked at her naivety. Surely she knew what danger she was in? Her reply wasn't going to wash. Younger members of her team were in agreement: there was only one way she could survive the attacks on her and that was to come out with a firm and fulsome apology. She should say she had been young and naive at the time, etc, but now she realised how inappropriate it had been for her to accept the money. She would make a large donation to a charity working with victims of climate change.

"But that would undermine my authority," Gregory told them. "They won't go away – they'll just keep on digging for more. Why oblige them?"

Her chief of staff spoke for all his colleagues. "Prime minister, you're going to lose this battle – and fast."

*

For two hours after the story broke, there was no public statement from Gregory's office. All the while, further accusations were being made on Mob. Unsubstantiated claims were being made – that Gregory had enjoyed flights at the oil company's expense, been entertained at the opera, taken to sporting events and put up at lavish hotels. What else had gone on? Was she still secretly being fed with ill-gotten money? Was she still in contact with the oil company's former executives who, following its bankruptcy, had fled the country, to locations unknown?

While there was no evidence of Gregory's continued contact with any Albion Oil executives, reporters did manage to uncover a letter in which Gregory thanked Albion Oil for the donation. There it was, in black and white. The whole country was commenting on it. And still there was no word from Number 10. Why not? Surely she wasn't going to deny it?

It was mid-afternoon when Gregory replied with a written statement, having decided – against her aides' advice – on a course of action that stopped short of an apology.

"About 15 years ago when I was a newly-elected MP," she wrote, "I was approached by Albion Oil and offered the small sum of £500 to help with the day-to-day costs of running my office. At the time I was finding my feet and any money was welcome. Obviously, with hindsight I recognise that I should not have taken money from an oil company, and in fact I accepted no further donations from this source. But those were different times, and the full consequences of climate change were not apparent. I hope that you will accept this as an explanation and we can lay this matter to rest."

It was, she soon realised, a forlorn hope. The statement merely encouraged further attacks. Leader of the opposition Jake Raglan quickly did what Gregory had failed to do: he summoned the TV cameras to add his comments live on air.

"Today we have heard an utterly unsatisfactory response from the prime minister. For years I have been aghast at this government's failure to speed up the transition to a zero carbon economy. How come we are even contemplating bringing diesel generators into the country when we are in a state of climate cataclysm? Now we know all too well. We have a prime minister who has been propped up with bribes from the evil merchants of death in the oil industry, and who claims she knew nothing about the climate cataclysm at the time. That's getting close to denial, that is."

*

Oblivious to all this was Bryan Geavis, sitting at home in Essex, still brooding over what he saw as a slight on his character by Suza Shamon. He had turned the television off halfway through the Evie Wilks interview, irritated by the way he thought she had evaded questioning by becoming emotional. Later he felt a little guilty for thinking this way – she had, after all, been through a traumatic experience. But still, it was alien to him to show such emotion in public – anger, perhaps, excepted. Maybe she should be allowed to emote, and he should just keep quiet.

But one thing he wasn't prepared to let go was the assertion on *The Suza Shamon Show* that he had been an imposter, a fraud, and not a professional meteorologist.

"I feel a fool," he told Olivia. "But how do I protest without letting them know my history, that I worked for an oil company?"

"You can't," she said. "So why not just let it go?"

"Because there are several million people out there who saw me last week and who think I was lying, that I weaselled my way onto the show just so that I could try to refute science. I can't live with that, even if I never want to show my face on television again."

"But I thought we'd made the decision to move to Brazil. You'll soon forget all about it."

"I need people to know I was a professional. I take pride in that. If I have to write and admit that I worked for an oil company, so be it. I've nothing to be ashamed of. I took great care with my work."

"Don't be so pig-headed. You'll just bring attention to yourself that you'll regret."

In the end, Geavis settled on a halfway house. No, he wouldn't contact Diversity TV directly. But he would write to Guy Hovis, head of the Agency for Modelling Climate Chaos, with whom he had worked many years ago, when they were both young meteorologists establishing their careers. Surely, Hovis would vouch for him as a professional – and without his having to disclose the identity of Geavis' employer.

He thought an email would be too impersonal, so he penned a letter instead – almost a quirky, eccentric thing to do now, as far as many people were concerned – reminding Hovis of their time together at what was then the Met Office. He felt in a positive mood as he went out to post the letter, and took a walk down to the sea front in a mild south westerly breeze. The conditions were so benign, he thought, that for once the weather would be off the front pages.

On his way back home he thought he caught sight of Bunty, but in such ragged clothes that he wondered what was up with her. She's gone off the rails, he told himself.

It wasn't until the morning that Geavis reconnected with the news. He switched on the television to see Sheila Gregory trying to answer reporters' questions – and struggling against voluminous shouting from a crowd on Whitehall.

"I have thought over it and have come to the conclusion that the answers I gave yesterday were unsatisfactory," she said. "This morning I want to give a fulsome apology for my actions 15 years ago. I now accept there was no excuse for accepting money from an oil company. I hope that in my favour people will take into account the considerable efforts I have taken to decarbonise Britain. There are no more oil companies in Britain, and that is a huge achievement. I am very sorry that my judgement failed me on that one occasion, 15 years ago, before the scale of the oil companies' contribution to climate crisis became fully apparent, and I hope now that we can draw a line under this matter."

Some hope. The cameras then cut to Evie Wilks, who was among a group chanting at the gates to Downing Street. "The prime minister is getting more two-faced by the hour," she said. "She tells us she's driven the oil companies out of business, and yet one of her own ministers has told us that the country is awash with secret installations of diesel generators. It doesn't take much to put two and two together: Sheila Gregory is a stooge for the oil industry. She is in its grubby hands. There's only one thing she can do now – and that is resign!"

A statement was soon released by the government, attempting to explain the situation. Yes, it confirmed, there were diesel generators: 6,000 of them spread around the country. But they were not used continuously, only intermittently when wind and solar energy was low. They were strictly an interim measure while greater energy storage facilities were developed – at which point the country would be able to exist solely on renewable energy. The diesel itself was imported under licence from other countries, via a route the government could not disclose.

"Keep it secret if you dare," came Evie Wilks' reply, "but we will find how that diesel is coming into the country – and we will stop it. We'll make you regret your dirty little pact with the devil."

Disturbingly, for Gregory's advisers, public opinion seemed to be moving with the protestors. "They're only making their point, aren't they?" said one woman interviewed on the street for the midday news. "What with all this weird weather we're getting, someone's got to do something about it, haven't they?"

A balding man in a suit was also asked for his opinion. "I would have sympathy for the prime minister accepting the money, because things were very different 15 years ago," he said. "But why does it take her so long to admit the truth? Her manner leaves a lot to be desired, I'm afraid."

Occupying one end of a long sofa in yet another crisis meeting in her Downing Street office, Gregory was beginning to lose heart.

"Is that really a reflection of the public's views?" she asked her two closest advisers. "How do we know they didn't interview 100 people and the other 98 said they agreed with what the government is doing?"

Her advisers looked at each other. "That's not quite a line we can take," one of them said. "We've got to accept how this is being perceived. Oil companies are now the bogeyman, whether we like it or not."

What would be fatal, they agreed, would be if the story were allowed to become a steady drip, drip, drip of revelations, day after day. Was there any more to come out?

Gregory was adamant there could not possibly be. "I only ever accepted one donation," she insisted. That reassured her team, but what was needed was a bold policy statement – something eye-catching that would put her accusers on the back foot.

Advisers racked their brains all afternoon. Gregory asked, should the government bring forward once again the target for eliminating carbon emissions altogether? Not dramatic enough. Could a few of the generators be symbolically decommissioned and dismantled – put beyond use? That received a warmer reception. But what won the day was a suggestion that the government should create a new criminal offence of five years in jail for anyone caught consorting with an oil company, or living on the earnings of an oil company – save, obviously, for the licensed trade to provide diesel for emergency generators and air fuel for aircraft used by climate influencers.

Gregory was delighted by the suggestion. Thoughts of resignation, which had been fluttering around her mind all day, were briefly put to rest.

But then doubts began to creep in. Was it a little bit over the top? Might good people go to jail as a result? She asked herself whether it was fair to single out oil company executives when they had only extracted the stuff from the ground; *everyone* had burned it. But these thoughts, too, were put to rest as she took a double whisky to her upstairs quarters and buried herself in a TV drama, her bare feet on the coffee table – a little act of rebellion, as she saw it, against the lack of privacy she suffered all day, every day.

The announcement of the new policy was scheduled for first thing in the morning.

What Gregory and her team hadn't reckoned with was that the wind would strengthen during the night and blow the roof off a block of flats on the Isle of Wight, killing two people and injuring 10 more. There were dramatic television pictures as rescue services fought to free the injured before the building collapsed altogether. Again, the weather forecasters had failed to foresee the severity of the storm – although several local residents suggested that the real cause might be shoddy workmanship.

"I've been saying for weeks that you could see daylight between the top of the wall and that flat roof," one woman told reporters. "It shouldn't have been like that, surely."

The following day, she received a letter from solicitors representing the developers who had built the flats, warning that they would be taking legal action if she repeated the claim. Terrified and suffering from palpitations, she kept quiet when reporters came calling for more evidence of the shoddy workmanship.

Instead, the *Daily Torrent* decided to focus on the climate angle. "Now it's Undeniable," read its headline the following day. "Second Violent Storm in a Month tips Britain's Climate into Meltdown."

And to think that the newspaper had once dismissed climate change as a great hoax, thought Sheila Gregory over breakfast, preparing for her showdown with the media. Her team was undecided as to whether the news overnight would hinder or help her. "I think it's good for us," said Gregory. "It takes a little attention away from the issue of the donation and reinforces the policy I am going to announce."

Her attitude worried her aides. "Well, don't sound *too* overjoyed," one said. "You've first got to acknowledge that people have died."

An hour later, Gregory was live on the radio.

"We've seen overnight the dreadful consequences of climate change," she said. "My heart goes out to the families of those who have been killed. My government is not going to stand still. Today, I am announcing new measures to crack down on those culpable for climate change, namely those in the oil industry who for years kept pumping the oil out of the ground when they knew the damage they were causing. As you know, I was myself a victim of their mendacity, and I am determined to root out those who are responsible for the crisis. We will redouble our efforts to hunt for missing oil company executives. In the meantime, we will speed a law through parliament which will introduce a mandatory five-year sentence for anyone found guilty of aiding and abetting the industry. There will be immunity for those involved in the strictly licensed trade in oil and gas products for exceptional purposes."

"Masterly," was the verdict delivered by Gregory's chief of staff. But now he and his colleagues would have to sit down and work out how the new penalties were actually going to be enforced. Civil servants were well aware that the country could not cope without a continuing import trade in oil and gas, but this was less well-known among the population at large. Without imported diesel, power distribution would fail completely. The nation was proving to be stubbornly dependent on fossil fuels. When the gas grid had been decommissioned it was on the assumption that giant batteries would soon become available to store several weeks' worth of energy, but the technology was taking longer to develop than had been anticipated. The problem that exercised officials in the Department for the Climate Crisis was this: if the government was threatening stiff new penalties for unlicensed traders and for those who had been part of the oil industry in the past, would it frighten the suppliers on whom the country still relied? Would they stop selling oil to Britain altogether?

But there was little time to worry about the details of the new laws, as the leaders of the Huddle for Love movement continued to agitate against the prime minister. They simply weren't going to give up. "How despicable that the prime minister should call herself a victim of the oil industry," announced Evie Wilks through a megaphone to an ever-growing mass of protesters in Whitehall. "The real victims are those lying beneath rubble on the Isle of Wight."

A little while later, a band of Greenshirts in Hertfordshire reckoned that they had found one of the secret installations of diesel generators. They hacked away at it and posted a video online. "For God's sake," Sarah Downwood told the cabinet that morning. "It's a good job that wasn't in use at the time or they'd have been barbecued. I know who would have been blamed then – and it wouldn't have been the protesters; it would have been us."

Emergency security arrangements were hastily made to protect the installations. This, however, created a new problem: the clusters of guards deployed in remote locations gave the Greenshirts a big clue as to where the installations were.

Matters didn't get any better for Sheila Gregory in the House of Commons. "So now we know," hissed Jake Raglan across the despatch box. "Yet again we have been deceived by this double-dealing government. They told us they were bearing down on carbon emissions. And now the truth slips out – that they are secretly burning fossil fuels beneath our noses. We have a prime minister who has taken the oil companies' shilling, and who now smuggles oil into the country on the quiet."

In vain did Gregory try to convince him and his MPs that the generators were essential if the country's electricity supply was not to collapse. Against jeering from across the chamber, she changed tack and reminded him of the announcement she had made earlier that morning: that oil company executives, other than those involved in licensed trade, would from now on face five years in jail.

"What a pitiful sentence for those who have brought death to our country," Raglan replied. "Just last night another two have died – victims of an industry that was evil beyond evil. And what does the government propose? The sort of prison sentence we give the poor and hungry for stealing food. It should be ten years at the very least!"

The killer blow, however, came not from Raglan but from an anonymous user on Mob who posted a photograph of the younger Sheila Gregory, in hard hat and overalls, at what looked like an oil refinery: you could see a mass of pipes behind her. Was it really an oil refinery? Gregory racked her brains to remember what the occasion was – she had visited so many places in her political career. Perhaps it was a chemical works in a marginal constituency she had passed by during an election campaign. Or could it have been a brewery? But no, she couldn't place the photo.

It proved to be a fatal lapse of memory.

"As if any more proof was needed," Evie Wilks told her crowd. "This is a prime minister who is up to the eyeballs in the oil industry. She takes its money, she fools us all into paying for its product and now we have a photograph of her consorting with the devil itself. That's five years in jail, according to your own law, Sheila!"

Raglan now stepped up the pressure, too, demanding Gregory's resignation. Finally, and most brutally, Zoe Fluff, waiting at Heathrow for a flight to the Seychelles, sent out a message on Mob. "Here am I, off to see the damage we've wrought on the disappearing beaches of the Indian Ocean. Can't say how ashamed I am that Britain's PM is the pay of the planet-wreckers."

Within minutes, several million were reading it. Gregory herself still wanted to tough it out but her ministers said no. Enough was enough. Either she went or she would bring the government down with her.

In tears, she walked from the front of Number 10 Downing Street to a forlorn lectern set out on the tarmac, as inviting as a gibbet. "For the past three years I have done my very best to address the climate crisis," she said as the camera flashes blinded her. "We are well on our way to hitting zero emissions. We have closed down the oil industry. We have switched off the gas supply. We have taken millions of cars off the road. What other prime minister in history can boast such a list of achievements? But it is clear to me now that I have lost the confidence of parliament and the country, and it would be better if it were left to others to continue this work."

Her statement over, she felt less tearful and more angry. What more could she have done? They were fools, those who had brought her down – they didn't understand the decisions she had had to make, the balances she had had to strike. How rich it was for the leader of the opposition to go on about the hungry – there would be far more people left cold and hungry if the generators were turned off. But it was no use her getting drawn into these kinds of thoughts. She knew that dignity demanded that she support her successor, and that she would have to regain her composure.

*

Watching the resignation on television at home in Essex, Bryan and Olivia Geavis were dispassionate.

"Never did like her much," said Olivia. "Arrogant, she was. And distant, too."

"I can't say I warmed to her. But what was it she did wrong?" said Geavis. "I'm not clear on that."

"Who cares? Someone's head had to roll. I'm fed up with the power cuts and I want someone to be accountable. If it's her, that's alright by me."

"But who are we going to get instead, eh? What makes you think they'll handle the situation any better?"

"Doubt if we'll notice the change much. They're all the same, politicians, aren't they?"

"We don't allow them to be any different. Box them in a corner and what do you expect?"

"They could try and inspire us."

"To do what?"

"Well, just inspire us..."

"Do we want inspiration from our leaders, or just competence?"

Olivia could find nothing to say in response. Why were these conversations so stale? How ironic that she damned politicians for being uninspiring, when she couldn't inspire her husband – and he couldn't inspire her.

How long had it been this way? She tried to remember whether their relationship had suddenly tailed off or whether it had been a gradual downhill slope. The history of their years together was lost in a fog of memories of unsatisfactory evenings. While Geavis drifted off to sleep that night, dreaming of more storms brewing in the Atlantic, Olivia almost began to envy Sheila Gregory for having a life change forced upon her.

Would her relationship improve when they got to Brazil?

5

The west-facing plate glass windows of Guy Hovis' twentieth-storey office were to him a private joke. It was as if the architect believed it would help the head of the Agency for Modelling Climate Chaos to be able to see the approaching weather, when in reality his forecasts were the work of computers concealed in the building's weatherless basement. But today of all days he felt that the scudding clouds, luminous from the city lights, really were an inspiration as he pondered the problem that had been bothering him.

Why, for the second time in a month, had his models failed accurately to predict the path and strength of a storm? Forecasts had improved so much over his long career – as the computational speeds had increased. How astonishing it would have seemed 40 years before that he could have forecast the formation of a depression which had yet to form. Yet his models had been tested by the conditions of the past few weeks and been found wanting. Events in the real atmosphere and those in the pretend, digital one created by his own technologists were beginning to diverge – or rather, to diverge far too soon. Three, five days into the future and it was only to be expected that the forecasts would often fail. But eight hours ahead? That ought to be well within the capability of his models. Somewhere, incorrect assumptions had been made, or a bug had entered his computers – so subtly that on some days it could seem as if nothing was wrong. But then, when it really mattered, the forecast was going awry.

Could it really be blamed on climate change, as he had himself suggested on television? The oceans were warming, to be sure, and harbouring extra energy. But this shouldn't have thrown his atmospheric models; there was something else wrong. How long would it take to fix? He hated to think that a third storm would catch the country unawares. So far, his organisation had got away with its two failures, without too many questions being asked. But with high pressure settled over Greenland there were going to be more storms in the near future, racing into the giant plughole that the North East Atlantic had become. Sooner or later, people were going to start asking serious questions about his organisation's competence – and Hovis' personal integrity, too.

Tired of looking for inspiration from the clouds, Hovis started looking around his desk instead. His eyes settled on a handwritten letter, which had been brought in with the post earlier that afternoon. Strange, he thought; who writes to me in pen and ink anymore?

It wasn't unknown for the agency to receive handwritten letters, usually from lonely, elderly people who had spotted the birds doing something unusual, or seen flowers and berries appearing at what they thought to be the wrong time of year – and wondering whether it presaged a season of unusual weather. These letters were sometimes pinned up on the wall for their entertainment value, but they never reached the top floor. So why was this one addressed to Hovis personally, and why had his PA decided that he ought to look at it himself?

The signature meant nothing to him at first, though it soon came back to him. Bryan Geavis: yes, that did ring a bell. A long time ago they were colleagues, until Geavis went off to work in the North Sea, attracted by higher earnings – going over to the dark side, Hovis thought at the time. Hovis himself had settled for what he saw as the more worthy option: working for a public agency.

Hovis had never come across Geavis in the four decades since, so what did he want now?

"I don't know if you were aware, but I appeared last week on *The Suza Shamon Show*, giving my views on weather forecasting and whether climate change is making it more difficult," the letter began. Now it came flooding back: yes, Hovis had received a report about this interview – it had caused a stir in the PR department of the Agency for Modelling Climate Chaos and for a couple of days there had been some debate whether or not to respond, but in the end staff had decided to ignore it.

It seemed that Geavis was asking a personal favour. "Last Sunday my name was slandered," the letter went on. "I was described as a fake meteorologist. As someone who knows the truth I would be hugely grateful if you would help set the record straight."

But there was a complication. Geavis only wanted the record set straight up to a point: he wanted Hovis to write a letter to Diversity TV, vouching that he was a genuine, professional meteorologist but not to give any details of his later career – i.e. Hovis was not to mention that he had worked for an oil company.

What a cheek, thought Hovis. Here was a sometime colleague who had gone on television to question the competence of the Agency for Modelling Climate Chaos, but who now wanted Hovis to intervene on his behalf. Was that reasonable? He was tempted to screw up the letter and set it flying across the room.

But then again, what would he have done in the same circumstances? Should he indulge his sometime colleague, or did he deserve to be cast loose, in punishment for attacking the Agency for Modelling Climate Chaos' forecasting skills?

Hovis dithered, quietly welcoming the distraction from the far greater problem which had been occupying him.

*

A couple of miles away across London, Amber was celebrating a landmark. For the first time she had been allowed to travel to central London without her parents. It had been her eleventh birthday a few days earlier and that had tipped the balance in her favour, made her parents relent and give permission. They had been reassured by the fact that she would be travelling with Misha, who was a year older and was considered by many parents at her school to be especially mature for her age.

But for Amber, this was not just a case of celebrating a new life of semi-independence; it was a calling. She was off to join the climate campaign in Trafalgar Square. She was certain that she had already helped to bring down the prime minister, by standing up and being counted. She had done her bit and made sure those filthy diesel generators from Spain never got to pollute the London air. She couldn't understand how Sheila Gregory had been so foolish as to sanction the burning of fossil fuels. Did she not understand the peril the Earth was in?

Night after night, Amber had been kept awake by fears for the planet's future. She knew, from what she had read, that big storms were coming, that fires were taking hold, that London, the only city in which she had ever lived, would soon disappear beneath the waves. How could Sheila Gregory live with herself, having allowed these generators to spew poison into the atmosphere?

But now Gregory was gone, and Amber, Misha and her friends felt jubilant. "We've done it!" said Misha, high fiving the other girls. "The world can breathe a little easier."

Or could it? In spite of the air of celebration in the crowd, Amber felt uneasy. Weren't there power stations and factories elsewhere in the world, still pumping out the deadly gases?

"Does it really mean the storms won't get worse now?" she asked Misha. "If they are still pumping out carbon dioxide in China, won't we get the storms anyway?"

Her friend was not in the mood for addressing this question. "Why don't we just enjoy this moment?" she said. "We've brought down one of the most powerful people in the world. If we can do that, we can do anything."

They said no more and instead listened to Evie Wilks.

"They're going to tell us who is going to be the new prime minister, but who cares? *We* are now the *real* government," Wilks said. An enormous cheer went up. "It's us who will make the real decisions, not the corrupt ministers who hide away in the Houses of Parliament. *This* is where the power now lies – out on the streets!"

*

The keepers of the constitution, however, had other ideas. On the advice of

Sheila Gregory, Sarah Downwood was summoned to Buckingham Palace and asked to form a government as interim prime minister. It took an hour and a half for police to clear a path for her car to get back to Downing Street. When she finally arrived, she managed only a few brief words, and even they were largely drowned out by the chants from protesters at the gates.

"I have been asked to form a government and have been delighted to accept," she said. "I don't have to tell you what my priority will be. This is no longer a crisis – it is more serious than that. If we do not act, everything we hold dear is in danger of being torn from us by runaway climate change. I promise I will not waste a minute. I will enact, as soon as practically possible, the measures that my predecessor announced yesterday morning. It will become a crime, punishable by up to five years in jail, to promote the continued use of fossil fuels. We will pursue with vigour oil company executives who have gone on the run. I can also announce that we will begin to decommission the diesel generators and speed up further the transition to zero carbon. To underline just how seriously my government will take this issue, I am bringing the Ministry for the Climate Crisis under my own wing. From now on, it will be known as the Ministry for the Climate Cataclysm."

Would that be enough to settle the protesters? Downwood wondered, as she turned and took the few steps back to her new front door. She was not sure what else she could do. Talks with her advisers revealed what she feared: to decommission generators would mean more and longer power cuts if the calm, overcast weather returned. In that case, the government risked more riots from the cold and hungry. The best the government could hope for was that the weather would continue as it was now: a conveyor of depressions rolling in from the mid-Atlantic, bringing plentiful wind to keep the turbines turning and enough hours of sunshine to keep the solar panels generating.

"If we can get through to March, the danger should be over," her chief adviser told her. "We would then have about seven months to work out what we need to do to prevent winter power cuts."

"And what are the options?" asked Downwood.

"That is a work in progress."

True to her word, Downwood introduced an emergency bill to parliament two days later to create new offences of encouraging, promoting or profiting from the fossil fuel industry. The law would be retrospective, to allow the prosecution of former oil company executives.

But Downwood knew this was not going to be enough in itself; to survive in office she would have to meet with the protesters who had brought down her predecessor and absorb some of their ideas. Extend a warn hand of welcome to them, she hoped, and she might just get them to turn a blind eye to the clause she knew would have to be included in her bill. This addition, which came to be known among her staff as the 'Sheila Gregory clause', would provide exemption for ministers and public officials who had worked with the oil industry in the past. It was necessary, Downwood argued, because politicians and civil servants had had to work with all sorts of people, from foreign dictators to oil company chiefs. It would be wrong for them to be held accountable for meetings they had held as part of their duties.

*

The invitation to 10 Downing Street, when it came, did not greatly impress Evie Wilks. She was not going to be starstruck by meeting the prime minister; already, in her own mind, Wilks was more powerful than the official leader of the country, so why the need for deference? Sarah Downwood, she reckoned, had about the same consistency as putty; she could be moulded as the Huddle for Love leaders saw fit. This would be true even if, as the letter of invitation made clear, only three members of the movement were being invited through the gates.

"Of course, I'd love 30 of us to encircle the prime minister," Evie told a meeting hastily arranged to consider the proposal. "But we should take it as a compliment, a sign of the PM's weakness, that she only feels safe with three of us."

But who should those three representatives be? Evie herself, obviously. A man called Firkin was quick to push himself forward for the second place. But the third?

There were plenty of candidates, each of whom claimed to have been instrumental in setting up the Trafalgar Square camp – a camp that had outgrown its original home and now snaked halfway down Whitehall. Should they send a loudmouth, a seasoned protester who had been arrested multiple times? They argued about gender balance; this was irreconcilable with just three places available, unless, it was suggested, they found a trans person. Then came a moment of inspiration from one of the candidates.

Why not send a child?

There would be nothing more disarming for the prime minister than to be put in her place by a child. It would be a no-win situation for Sarah Downwood: if she ignored, rejected or attacked the child's ideas in any way she would stand accused of patronising the entire Huddle for Love movement. The climate cataclysm put children's futures at stake; there was no way Downwood could refuse to recognise that.

An announcement was made to the camp: would a child come forward and volunteer? Most who went forward were 17 or even 18: obstreperous teenagers who had assumed the attitude of Evie, Firkin and many others. Amid these wannabe revolutionaries, Misha at once stood out for her innocence; the moment the ruling committee saw her small round glasses it was almost inevitable that she would end up being chosen.

"What is the first thing you would tell the prime minister?" she was asked.

"I'd say, 'you can ignore me if you want, but it's me who will be writing the history books long after you have gone. And you won't get a good write-up if you don't listen to me now.'"

The committee smiled, and she was officially chosen a few moments later.

On the morning of the following Monday, the Downing Street gates were swung back a few degrees and the trio made their way up the short street, the camera crews delighted by what looked like a strangely-inverted family of scruffy, rebellious parents and their smartly-dressed child. While the trio posed for photographs, Evie made a short speech in which she did not repeat her claim to be "the real government" but told reporters that "we are not going to be leaving empty-handed. We owe it to future generations not to waste a moment."

The meeting had been stage-managed so that the protesters would not be allowed beyond a ground floor meeting room and were accompanied at all times by a dozen security guards. But this seemed unnecessary, as the protesters were displaying remarkably good behaviour. The only thing, thought Downwood, was that they did smell a little; she tried hard to disguise her repulsion. The burly security guards looked ridiculous alongside Misha, something the girl herself used to her advantage.

"What did you think I was going to do, set upon you with my claws?" she asked, to which Downwood replied with an uncomfortable laugh.

The meeting had been scheduled to last three-quarters of an hour, and Downwood assumed it would be a polite affair, in which she would explain what the government was doing and invite a few suggestions for consideration in future legislation.

Evie, Firkin and Misha, however, were not going to be fobbed off so easily. Yet, they did not try to accost the prime minister or talk over her; rather, they wore her down by their unexpected mildness. "I had prepared for them to be lippy," Downwood later told her confidants. "I was up for that. Instead I found myself walking on eggshells, so pleased by their sweet reasonableness that I became fearful of saying something that would make them turn."

Downwood began the meeting by repeating everything she had mentioned on the steps of Downing Street a few days earlier. "As you can see, we are far from idle," she said. "But of course it is important that we bring the people with us, which is why I have asked you here today – to see if you have any ideas."

The prime minister had been expecting a mini manifesto, perhaps including a couple of ideas which she might adopt in some way. But Evie had worked out that her best strategy, now she had her foot in the door, was to concentrate on keeping it there.

"Yeah, we've got loads of stuff," she said. "But this relationship isn't going to work unless you give us a permanent role in government. What we're demanding is a citizens' cabinet, where you consult us on every policy that could affect the climate."

"An ongoing dialogue?" said Downwood. "Yes, that is a good idea. We should certainly continue to meet."

"We'd need a veto," said Firkin.

"A *veto*?"

"On everything."

"But parliament has the final say."

"But you need to be sure about what you're putting before parliament. That it's legitimate, I mean."

"That it's legitimate?"

"You have to understand, prime minister, that we're just representing the people. There's 100,000 people out there on the streets and they need to be represented. It's not what I say; it's not what Evie or Misha says. There's a swell of people out there, and parliament needs to know that what you're putting to it is legitimate."

"But we have a cabinet to decide that."

Wilks gave Downwood a friendly but piercing look.

"And how many of the cabinet, I wonder, have been compromised in the way that Sheila Gregory was? There could be much more to come out. It would be far more sensible if you co-operated with us."

Downwood suddenly got it. She thought back through her career, trying to remember every donation she had accepted, every meeting she had held. Did Wilks already have evidence linking her in some oblique way to the oil industry? She couldn't decide, but a few minutes later, Downwood had conceded the principle of a citizens' cabinet, which would meet every fortnight with the official cabinet.

But there was more to come. Misha, who had been quiet so far, then spoke up.

"For climate crimes we think you shouldn't have the ordinary courts, with all the wigs and all that," she said. "They just let all the climate deniers off. We need a special climate court. Because these crimes affect young people like me more than they do old people, it's *us* who should decide whether someone is guilty or not."

"You mean a jury of young people?" said Downwood.

"Yes, a jury of the future. Do you like that idea?"

"It's interesting."

"Shall we agree on it, then?"

"Well…"

"I've got another idea, too. Your new law about aiding and abetting oil companies: what is 'aiding and abetting' supposed to mean? It would make much more sense if you had a law against stealing a child's future – because that's exactly what these oil executives have done. It's *our* futures, *our* dreams that are being taken away as the planet is destroyed. You've all had your lives, but we haven't had a chance."

Downwood raised her eyebrows. "Why, that's a fantastic idea! Simple, and well… straight to the point."

Within a few moments, Downwood had agreed to both proposals. She genuinely liked them, thought them imaginative. The symbolism would be fantastic. And wouldn't it help her party win back some of the youth vote?

It was only later that she and her advisers started to struggle with the details of how a child jury would work. Were under-18s really mature enough to sit on juries? And who would advise them, make sure that they understood the process and the concepts of what was being discussed?

But these are details, she comforted herself, and of course they can be fixed. The important thing was that she had made a statement and got the Huddle for Love protesters onside. That, surely, was where Sheila Gregory had failed. There was a way ahead. She could govern.

Or so she thought.

Over the next few days, the citizens' cabinet made a number of suggestions, all of which were accepted by Downwood. But one of them was to have more lasting repercussions than any other.

Wilks, worried that the 35 victims of the Guy Fawkes Night storm were beginning to fade from public consciousness, demanded that the government publish a daily total of people deemed to have died as a result of the effects of the climate cataclysm. The numbers were to be calculated by a team of academics appointed by the Huddle for Love leaders.

Downwood was well aware that such figures might be used against her government, but was reassured when the initial toll seemed quite low. On the first day it was just six – all elderly people who had succumbed to chest infections said to have been caused by the recent fog. This statistic did not, initially, attract much comment. But day by day the number grew, and public attention seemed to grow with it.

A week later the daily toll had climbed to 23 – and included such people as a cyclist thrown off his bicycle by a pothole allegedly created by unusual levels of rain and frost, a woman allergic to bee stings who had been stung by a creature considered to be unusually active for the time of year and a woman in Wales trampled to death in the street by a herd of wild cattle – animals which had been released from a bankrupt dairy farm years before and had been living on the hillsides but, unable to find good winter pasture, had descended upon a nearby village.

In parliament, the daily death toll was frequently quoted back at Downwood by the leader of the opposition, Jake Raglan.

"You preside over a rising toll of death and destruction. It's blood on your hands. What are you going to do about it?"

In vain did Downwood try to reply that the daily total of people killed by the climate cataclysm was an experimental statistic, and that it was only being published because the government cared so much. Raglan would always get up again.

"These are real people," he would say. "Fathers, mothers, sons and daughters. They're not mere statistics to be played around with by this callous government."

Much as Downwood tried to dismiss these exchanges as part of the cut and thrust of parliament, the daily statistic gained traction. It did not matter how tenuous she thought the connection between some of the deaths and the climate cataclysm, the only thing apparently absorbed by the general public was the concept of a rising death toll caused by climate change. The figure started cropping up in public conversation and in radio and television interviews. People who previously might have objected to some of the measures to tackle the climate cataclysm, perhaps by grumbling about the need to fill in a quarterly carbon return, became more reluctant to do so, knowing that they would be accused of not caring about the 30 or 40 people killed every day by people's selfish behaviour.

Downwood responded to the rising death toll by announcing tougher policies: a crackdown on people with open fires, a limit on the number of train tickets individuals could buy in any one year, a ban on barbecues. But still the death toll rose.

"Are we sure we have the right criteria?" she asked the citizens' cabinet in desperation. "Can the death of someone who drowned on a beach while swimming drunk after a night out *really* be blamed on stronger waves caused by climate change?"

Wilks was incredulous. "It's not going to look very good if it gets out that you've been trying to fiddle the figures. What do you think?"

Downwood said no more, but was struck by the realisation that trying to govern in tandem with the citizens' cabinet was going to be much harder than she had realised.

But how to tackle its influence when it had already burrowed its way so deeply into the furniture of government?

6

Geavis' mind was full of the climatic zones of Brazil as he set off on his afternoon walk to the seafront. Would he and Olivia take to the arid coastal regions near Rio or would they be better going further down into the country's subtropical tail, where the winters were wetter but the summers more bearably cool? The word 'cool' was of course relative; save for the occasional tropical downpour, they would be living in brightness, warmth and colour, so different from the low rainfall yet damp dreariness of south Essex. There would be hot sun, then brief evenings as the sun dived almost vertically towards the horizon, giving way to balmy nights and ever-so dark skies. He could hardly wait.

Geavis kept on thinking about the climate of Brazil until he reached the seafront, where he found himself instead, almost involuntarily, counting a flock of geese. Thirty-five, 36, 37… and was that a thirty-eighth he had missed as it passed behind one of the others? Why did he have the compulsion to count things? It hardly mattered how many geese were there, only the date of their migration: useful data which could be married with his records of temperature, rainfall and the budding and flowering of his roses and other garden plants. Maybe, when he reached Brazil, he would devote some time to writing a history of the climate of the Thames Estuary – how wonderful it would be to do that while enjoying the Brazilian sun! But this thought faded as he then found himself counting small boats on the estuary. Fifteen in all, he thought.

Why all this counting? He came to the conclusion that he was doing it because, for the first time in weeks, he was relaxed – happy, even. He counted things when he had nothing else to worry about or fill his mind.

On the way back home, he started counting gateposts. There were at least 55 separating his street from the seafront, though he never quite finished counting them, because a few yards from home he encountered Bunty, in another of her ragged jumpers.

Her reaction to seeing him caught him unawares.

"You disgust me!" she shouted. "How could you?"

What on earth was she on about? The obvious thing would have been to ask her, but Geavis couldn't quite bring himself to do so. Instead, he walked on, continuing to wonder about her outburst for the remaining few yards back to his front door.

About half an hour after getting home, the reason for Bunty's reaction became clear. Geavis looked at his phone to find it full of messages.

"Have you seen this?" one of them asked straightforwardly, referring him to a story on *The Progressive* website, with the title: "Suza's Fake Meteorologist was Oil Company Stooge." There was no doubt that it referred to Geavis. There was even a photograph of him, standing beneath the banner of Albion Oil in a PR photograph taken shortly before his retirement several years before. He remembered the occasion: he was launching a project to rewild the site of a former oil refinery, to create a new wetland for birds. But the context of the photograph was obscured for a casual viewer: the only thing people saw was that Geavis had once worked for an oil company – a simple fact that was soon to make his life intolerable.

The onslaught of posts on Mob exceeded everything he had endured a couple of weeks earlier.

"Oil company still trying to fight climate science from beyond the grave," read one.

"Despicable propaganda of many who claimed to be meteorologist," read another.

A few hours later, a reporter found his way to Geavis' front door. He answered, to be met with a camera flash and a question. "So, what have you got to say about your oil company links?"

When Geavis quickly shut the door, the reporter shouted his question through the letter box instead. The reporter received no reply, and went away to write a story titled "Could Oilman be First to Fall Foul of New Law?"

Within hours, Geavis and Olivia had reached the conclusion that they needed to leave their home – at least for a few days, until everything had settled down. Adam invited them to stay at his flat, although he knew it would be a bit of a crush.

"I wish you'd never gone on that damn programme," he told his father. "But the damage has been done, and the least I can do is offer you somewhere to stay for a few days."

Geavis and Olivia arrived in Beckton later that day, intent on trying to disrupt their son's family life as little as possible – and to spend their time preparing for the move to Brazil.

They had made some progress on this. They decided not to draw attention to themselves by applying for permission to take one of the few remaining direct flights; instead, they would travel by train through Europe, then take a boat to North Africa. According to their research, there were still flights from Morocco to Brazil – services that were open to anyone, in spite of pressure on governments all around the world to curtail airline travel. In all, it would take four or five gruelling days to reach Brazil, but it wasn't as if this was to be a regular journey. Once in South America they intended to turn their backs on Britain for good. They wouldn't be the only ones. Many others had begun to flee what they saw as rapidly declining living standards at home.

"It is so obvious that we are getting poorer as a country," said Olivia over dinner around a cramped dining table. "It is self-inflicted misery. And the worst thing is that we are not even allowed to know how bad things are – not since the government stopped publishing figures on economic growth. It's no longer relevant, they tell us – it's their national happiness index we should be taking notice of. Call me cynical, why does the happiness index keep going up? Who have they been asking? Not me. I think we were all a damn sight happier when the economy was growing."

"Oh, for sure," said Geavis. "I know we're supposed to be more fulfilled living close to nature and all that, and don't get me wrong – no-one likes a walk along the seafront more than I do, watching the birds. But there are so many things which we had when we were younger that people just don't have anymore. The chance to get in a car and drive wherever you want, the chance to eat food flown in from around the world, and fly off to places to explore them. You just don't have that now, do you?"

"But I'll tell you one thing," said Olivia. "They have a different attitude in Brazil. Does Tamsin message you much? Life seems to be one big party out there – even though they're supposed to be curtailing their emissions, like us. I don't know how they do it. Must be some naughtiness going on, I guess!"

"I'm sure there is. Maybe it's best not to ask too many details of how they do it, but all I can say is that I'd rather be out there enjoying myself rather than living a life of environmental purity here."

*

Later on, Geavis and Olivia both wondered if they had gone too far. They had been stressed by their experience of being abused on Mob. They were opening up, letting out their frustrations while looking ahead to their new life in Brazil. Maybe it had been rude of them to do so in front of Adam, Chloe and Amber, especially given that Adam and his family were not going to be sharing their adventure. But even so, they couldn't account for the reaction they had provoked. Amber's face turned red as she started to fidget with knives, forks, anything on the table.

It was her mother, however, who spoke first.

"How can that give you pleasure, going to live in a country that is cheating the system?" she said.

"We didn't say they're definitely cheating the system," said Geavis. "We don't know. I'm sure they're doing their best to cut emissions. All we're saying is that life is better there and so that's where we'd rather be."

"If life is good there now, it won't be for long. It'll be boycotted, and then what?"

"I think Brazil can cope by itself. It has the resources."

Amber could contain herself no longer. "It's horrible that you're even

90

thinking like that," she said, standing up and taking a couple of steps back. "We've only got one world and we're trashing it. How can you live with yourselves? There's people dying and you are just thinking of your own selfish little comforts. I'm ashamed to have you as my grandparents."

"Amber!" said Adam, as if in a half-hearted attempt to calm her down, though deep down he thought he sympathised a little more with his daughter than with his parents.

"But it's here in Britain that people are dying," said Olivia, "not because of climate change but because of our ham-fisted efforts to deal with it. People can't keep warm anymore. You never used to get all these people dying of bronchitis."

"And what of the fires?" said Amber. "What about the people being burned to death in them? And the people starving because the harvests have failed? There were 55 people killed today by climate change in Britain alone."

"But harvests have always failed," said Geavis. "They are failing a lot less now than when I was young."

"You make me sick. You just don't care! The fires are raging in Brazil – I've seen it on Mob. I hope that when you get there, they burn you both to a horrible death!"

"Amber!" said Chloe. "Please don't come out with that!"

But Amber was gone, back to her room, where she lay on the bed and picked up the book she had been reading earlier about animals affected by climate change. She reached the page with the pictures of the burned koala and started sobbing. *Why don't adults care?*

"I'm sorry," Adam told his parents. "She's getting a bit too passionate. There's good things to be said for that, I suppose. But it gets a bit out of hand sometimes."

It was some time before Geavis and Olivia spoke, and when they did, they stuck to small talk. The following day, having slept on the matter – and on an uncomfortable living room sofa – they were agreed: it would be better if they didn't stay at the flat. Adam said he wasn't going to ask them to leave but that perhaps they were right – the flat was a bit overcrowded and Amber, who was going through a bit of a difficult patch, needed space.

That afternoon, before Amber had returned from school, Geavis and Olivia took their bags and went out to look for a hotel.

It proved unexpectedly hard. They found a bland hotel in the old docklands but were turned away. "You're blocked," the receptionist told them. "Don't know why."

Geavis protested: "But there's plenty of money in my account!"

The receptionist shook his head. "Oh, it's not the payment that's the problem. It seems to be an issue with your social pledge. Can't tell you why." Couldn't he sign it again? "Won't let you. Just says you're blocked."

Geavis and Olivia went to another hotel, and the same happened. In the third hotel, Geavis took the initiative and suggested that he needed to sign the social pledge afresh. He went through, ticking the questions, but when it came to entering his name and date of birth, up came the words 'not valid'.

"What does that mean? How can I not be valid?" he asked.

"That's what it says when the system's decided that you've broken the contract," said the receptionist. What could he do about it? "Don't know. Never had someone like you before."

It seemed that Geavis had been reported by somebody, and the administrators of the social pledge had judged him to have broken the agreement he had signed weeks earlier. He had been frozen out of buying goods and services from any company that used the social pledge.

They eventually found a hotel, but only by using Olivia's credit card – and falsifying Geavis' name.

"What can I do?" Geavis asked his wife in despair, as soon as the door of their small room fell shut behind them. "At least if I had broken a criminal law I would be able to defend myself. But this? I don't even know who to protest to."

He hardly dared to switch on the news. Would he be on it? He hated to think, and perhaps it would be better if he shielded himself from news, as Olivia wanted him to do. But no, he couldn't rest until he was reassured there was nothing about him. He felt like public enemy number one: forced out of his home, verbally attacked by his own granddaughter and now banished from buying a hotel room and a meal.

But when he switched on the news there was nothing about him. How silly, he felt, even to think there would have been. Was he becoming paranoid?

Feeling relieved not to hear his name, the news hardly registered. Had he paid more attention, he would have learned that the Climate Changes Offences Bill had passed its second reading in parliament, after a heated debate in which the opposition had argued that the government should have gone further, much further. By the end of the debate two amendments had been added. The government itself – after consultation with the newly-established citizens' cabinet – had decided that two more offences should be added to the statute book. A clause should be inserted to allow for former oil executives to be charged with the manslaughter of anyone proven to have died as a result of climate change. There would also be a new offence of ecocide – to be defined as causing the death of a significant number of creatures by destruction of their habitat, and punishable with up to 10 years in jail.

Jake Raglan's opposition felt wrong-footed by the government's announcement. What could they do to make the government look inadequate, when it was clear that the measures represented a big step forwards? After a huddle of opposition spokesmen, Raglan took to the despatch box.

"The government has been pussyfooting on this endlessly," he said, thumping the box itself. "While the proposals for an offence of ecocide are welcome, what message does it send that they are proposing only a 10-year jail sentence for those found guilty? It is utterly wrong that the lives of other species should be officially judged to be worth so little compared with humans, when it is us who are responsible for their suffering? In the name of equality between the species we demand that the sentence for ecocide matches that of human murder – that is, jail for life."

His proposal was cheered by his own MPs. The government remained quiet, though one of its own backbenchers spoke against the amendment. "Are we not pushing this a little too fast? Can't we just wait to see how the new law beds in before we start imposing life sentences? I mean, as it reads at the moment, it looks as if I could end up in jail for the rest of my days for destroying a wasps' nest."

Sarah Downwood, worried how his intervention might play with the citizens' cabinet, whom she had agreed to brief the next day, muttered to one of her colleagues: "The usual suspect! I do wish he'd shut up." A few minutes later she agreed to write the life sentence into law – and the bill passed by 620 votes to three.

Evie Wilks and her citizens' cabinet cheered their success, but they were determined not to rest. They wanted to make sure the new law was going to be used, that it was not just some political gesture. Before the campfire in Trafalgar Square they agreed that it was essential to have a test case before too long, and they began to think of possible victims.

Attention swiftly turned to one name: that of Tyra Gaunt, the former *Daily Torrent* columnist. She had gone quiet for a while, but in recent weeks had started to write her own blog. Offensive as ever, she had had much to say about the Huddle for Love camp and the citizens' cabinet.

"Must be something we can get her for," said Firkin, scrolling through her latest writings. "What about this?" He read bits out: "Why I'm not taking lessons in how to live from this bunch of militant toerags… they claim to value the environment but look what they've done to their own environment. Trafalgar Square has become a steaming cesspit. Who dares go near the place now?… Filthy revolutionaries set up camp to protest about diesel fumes – and then spewed out far fouler smells themselves… Let's clear these ecofascists away before they make life unbearable for ordinary Londoners."

Her writings had been concocted to enrage the protestors, to be sure. But, as the Huddle for Love camp's lawyers pointed out again and again, there was nothing incriminating. Gaunt had honed the art of offending people over many years, and knew how to do so without getting herself into too many legal problems.

The following day, Sarah Downwood, who had travelled to South Wales to close a steelworks, was herself asked about the possibility of prosecuting Gaunt.

"No-one should be under any illusions about our determination to tackle not just climate change denial, but anyone who has aided and abetted the polluters," she explained. "But that doesn't mean we can simply prosecute anyone we like, no matter how offensive they have been towards members of the citizens' cabinet, with whom I am very proud to work."

When one reporter asked whether her reluctance was proof that the new law was purely token, she raised her voice. "Look, for the moment let us simply celebrate why we are here today: to close down these steelworks and with it make one more giant step towards Britain becoming carbon-neutral. That is a very real achievement, and one from which no-one should try to detract."

One lone reporter was unconvinced. "Given that we are going to have to import all our steel from now on, aren't we just shifting carbon emissions abroad?"

"For goodness' sake, can't you just accept good news when you hear it?" Downwood sighed. "In closing this plant, we are making a very clear statement of direction. Yes, it is true that there will have to be some imports in the immediate future, but we expect to see new miracle materials under development before too long."

As she was asked for details, Downwood was ushered away, back to her car, to be driven past a couple of hundred workers who had lost their jobs, some of whom were now being promised 'green jobs' assessing carbon emissions instead.

"This place was my life," one said tearfully. "The very least she could have done was to stop and speak to us directly."

*

The following day, Geavis and Olivia felt confident enough to go back home. They were several doors away when they noticed that something wasn't quite right. All of the front windows had been broken. Roses had been ripped away from the front of the building, some of their stems severed. "Where are you hiding, denier scum?" was scrawled across the brickwork.

"All this for standing up for meteorology," sighed Geavis as they picked through the broken glass.

They called the police, and an officer was sent to take swabs, collect what evidence there was. "Not much here," she said. "There's several bricks and

95

a garden gnome inside the property, which appear to have been used to break the windows. But no fingerprints on them. Any idea why someone should have attacked your property in this way?"

When Geavis told her about his difficulties, her manner changed appreciably. "Oh, Greenshirts," she said. "Don't think there's much point pursuing it in that case."

"Why on earth not?" asked Olivia. "It's our house, smashed – made uninhabitable."

"We have to proceed very carefully with the Greenshirts," said the officer. "They claim immunity on the grounds of conscience. It's been established in several cases, now. They say they acted as they did because it's a matter of human survival, and the courts swallow it. So long as they avoid injuring and murdering people, they're going to get off. Sorry to have wasted your time." And she was gone.

Over the next few days Geavis and Olivia had much business to see to. The windows had to be repaired, the graffiti removed and the roses reattached to the house. "That's what hurts me most," said Geavis. "They claim to be on the side of nature and yet they show such contempt for plants."

It did occur to him as he said it, though, that actually his roses weren't really natural, and, sure enough, when he looked up the Greenshirts online he discovered that 'rewilding' public and private gardens was a favourite tactic of theirs. "We're not going to be making any apologies for decolonising the natural world," one masked figure had told reporters after a municipal garden was ruined. "If we have to destroy every fucking bedding plant, we will."

The Greenshirt's words had led one columnist to comment: "The obsession with attacking tidy gardens just shows who these people are – spoiled kids reacting against their bourgeois upbringing." These were words some of his readers condemned as "frivolous in the face of a global emergency".

Olivia messaged Tamsin, informing her of their plans; Tamsin messaged back saying she couldn't wait to see her parents, that she had been looking into some temporary accommodation for them and that she was sure they would love it in Brazil.

Geavis and Olivia decided that they would rent out, rather than sell, their house. "Just in case it doesn't work out," Geavis suggested. They had estate agents round, followed by half a dozen viewers, one of whom signed a rental contract for a full year.

"That was easy," said Olivia. "That'll pay our way in Brazil. Maybe this will go better than we thought."

They sent a message to Adam and said they would contact him again when they reached Brazil. Wouldn't it be wonderful if the whole family could meet up again in Brazil at some point, wrote Olivia, though she quietly doubted this could happen. Leaving half her family behind was the one regret she had about emigrating – especially as they had not had the chance to patch things up with Amber. Should they have made more of an effort?

"Best not to contact her just at the moment," Geavis said. "We'll make up with her when we get to Brazil. It will be easier then, when we're not face to face."

Geavis and Olivia were unaware that Adam and Chloe were seriously worried about Amber's state of mind. She was becoming withdrawn, could not sleep and her schoolwork was suffering. She fussed over every last item of food, refusing to eat it unless she could be convinced that it was 'pure' – that no creature, nor ecosystem, had come to harm in producing it.

After a week of this, her parents took her to see a fashionable psychologist.

"She seems traumatised," Chloe said. "She was never like this before she came into contact with climate activism. We've tried to distract her, but we just can't. If only we could find something – *anything* – music, art, dancing, whatever –to take her mind off the climate."

The psychologist listened intently and then said, most directly and assuredly, that Chloe and Adam had been failing because they had got completely the wrong idea. "There is nothing irrational in your daughter's behaviour," she said. "She is concerned because she has very good reason to be concerned. She has great insight into the crisis of the climate. What is causing her such stress is her feeling that others around her do not share her feelings. What you need to do is to encourage her activism. You need to show that you, too, are fearful about the climate cataclysm. Cry with her over the dying animals. The three of you should go on a march, together. That will draw her back closer to you." Chloe and Adam doubted this would work, but having paid what they thought a handsome sum for the advice, were determined to give it a try.

Oblivious to all this, Geavis and Olivia busied themselves with wrapping up their lives in Essex and making final preparations for the journey. There was packing to do, but not much.

"New life, new start," said Geavis. "We don't need to be weighed down with baggage, real or metaphorical."

What they could not fit into four packing cases was stuffed up in the loft. But he did find room in his luggage for his handwritten weather records – of no practical use in Brazil, of course, but a reminder of his life's work. How fascinating it would be to compare the rhythms of the year wherever in Brazil they ended with those of the Thames Estuary.

They tried not to listen to the news. Too depressing, they told each other. "I'm demob happy," Geavis said over breakfast on the day before they left. "I'm not interested in what goes on here anymore. What a wonderful feeling it is to tune out of all the petty politics and goings on. You don't realise how much it all drags you down."

They were still avoiding the news the next morning, when an electropod arrived to take them to the station. This time, even that went smoothly. They took the train to London and changed there for Dover. They sent what they intended to be their last message to Adam from British soil and watched the passing countryside, green from recent rain. So English, they thought. Then they turned off their phones.

Thus, they were not to know that Geavis' name had surfaced as a possible test case for the new climate crimes law; a test case the prime minister and citizens' cabinet so badly wanted to bring. They were not aware that he had, out of nowhere, become the person most discussed on Mob. They had no idea that Zoe Fluff, off in the Galapagos Islands, had sent a message to her 18 million followers saying: "Makes me weep to see how the climate cataclysm has affected these beautiful islands. The tortoises look so sad and careworn. Must keep pursuing the people responsible for this. Oilman who disguised himself as meteorologist must be tried for killing the planet."

They had no way of knowing that at the highest levels in the Metropolitan Police, officers were discussing how to respond to the intense political pressure they felt to bring the first prosecution under the new law, and whether the man identified on Mob was a suitable candidate.

The first time Bryan Geavis knew he was being targeted was at passport control at the port of Dover, when he placed his passport face down on the glass and heard a loud alarm go off. Several staff hurried over at once.

The most senior took a look at his passport and said sternly: "Mr Geavis, you had better come with me."

7

The morning after Geavis' arrest, the newspapers seemed to know a remarkable amount about him. "Climate Arrest" read the headline on the *Daily Facsimile*. "Alleged Oil Executive Picked Up at Dover 'Ran PR Operation at Albion Oil'. Faces 10 Years for Role in Guy Fawkes Night Storm". The *Daily Torrent*, as ever, was more assertive and carried a photograph of Geavis at a company event several years earlier. "Justice for the Deptford Dead? Fleeing Oilman Snatched at the Border on Way to South America." Inside were five pages of photographs and text, put together from old press releases in which Geavis had featured, and several interviews with his neighbours. "Creepy Geavis kept himself to himself," was one sub headline. "Loved to tend his roses as world descended into climate chaos. Neighbours unaware of dark secret until he blew his cover with provocative TV interview in which he allegedly questioned climate change."

On Mob, the chatter was even less restrained, stripped of the 'allegedly' carefully placed by the professional media in their own headlines. "You took the oil money, sicko," wrote one. "Now you pay the price". Another read: "Earth may be on fire, but it still ain't as hot as where you're going, matey."

At the climate camp in Trafalgar Square, a huge cheer went up when the news came through. "This is for Deptford," an emotional Evie Wilks told the crowd. "How many years has it taken to get the culprits responsible for the climate cataclysm to face up to what they've done to the planet? Well, today, one man's luck has run out. Let's not waste it!"

Geavis knew nothing of what was being said about him. He had no access to news. An initial flush of bewilderment at his arrest soon gave way to anger and then to resignation. He remembered how, during idle moments in recent weeks, he had often imagined himself being arrested. After a day in custody, he began to feel an odd sense of relief. He now realised that, for the past few days, he had felt as if he was on the run. But now there was no reason to look behind him, no need to worry about the details of their interrupted journey; all was now superfluous. He slept more soundly than he had done for weeks – in spite of a hard bed.

He had to be woken for the first of what seemed interminable interviews. After a night in a cell in Dover he was handed over to the recently established climate crimes unit at Scotland Yard. It was known to have attracted some of the brightest and most ambitious police officers, who had correctly worked out that climate crimes were attracting special notoriety, and that the officers charged with investigating them would be in the limelight.

The police were especially interested in the last three years of Geavis' career at Albion Oil, when he worked in the company's PR department, specifically charged with organising coverage for climate-related initiatives.

"Albion Oil thought it could overcome growing hostility to its business by ploughing some of its profits into nature conservancy," Geavis explained to the officers. "It owned a number of coastal sites which had become surplus to requirements and which it sought to sell off for development. But it held back some of the land so that it could rewild it – or prove its green credentials, you might say. The company wanted everyone to know about these sites, which is why it set up a well-staffed PR office to publicise them. Some called it 'greenwashing', but I think that was a bit cynical. These places had become dead, toxic, but after restitution they were attracting an impressive range of birds."

It did not occur for a moment to Geavis to lie about any of this, not so much because he was afraid of being caught out or because he thought it would be immoral not to tell the whole truth, but because he thought the facts would help him. The new climate law, as far as he could make out, was not intended to capture the small cogs of oil corporations – from what he had understood, lowly employees were considered victims, not perpetrators. It was intended only to capture the senior managers – those who were responsibility for company policy and for directing large numbers of staff. And that wasn't me, thought Geavis.

"I never sought to work in PR," he said. "I was a meteorologist. But with declining operations in the North Sea, my post had become redundant. I was offered this job as a kind of wind-down to retirement."

The officers, who had been happy to allow Geavis to expand, calculating that giving him the chance to speak would relax him and open him up, then asked a direct question.

"And what was your official rank?"

"Rank?" said Geavis. "We weren't the police force. We didn't have ranks."

"Were you management, or not?"

"That is a bit of a grey area. My job in PR was really a sideways move, but in recognition of my long years of service it was arranged that I should be given what was technically a promotion – even if, in reality, I had no greater responsibility than I had before. I had less, in fact. As a meteorologist I had the lives of men in my hands. It wasn't like that in PR. All I really did was write press releases and show journalists and dignitaries around a reconstituted salt marsh, pointing out wading birds at every possible opportunity."

"You haven't answered my question. Were you management, or not?"

"Well, yes, technically I was a manager. But I'm not sure you could say I really managed anyone at all."

"Did you attend meetings?"

"I had to meet with people, yes."

"At what level? Did you meet the CEO?"

"I certainly met him once. I was asked to make a presentation on our environmental programme at the company AGM."

The longer the interviews went on, the more uneasy Geavis began to feel. He was trying to be helpful, yet he was being steered in a direction that felt uncomfortable. He was worried, too, about Olivia. Where was she? How was she handling it all?

When he asked the officers about his wife, he received no satisfactory reply. Were they being evasive because they were trying to hide something? Was Olivia okay? At the end of the second day he was surprised suddenly to be told that she was waiting to see him and that he could spend a few minutes with her.

For a while, they just looked at each other. Olivia wanted to be closer to her husband, but could not get over the suspicion that he had been hiding something from her – that he had committed a dreadful crime and concealed it for years. He seemed unable to convince her that, as far as he was concerned, he had committed no crime and was merely caught up in a little difficulty that would soon be resolved.

"When we get to Brazil, we'll laugh about this," he said.

"Will we?"

"Why not? The pressure will be off and we'll have a new life ahead of us."

Olivia fell silent again. She had tried to imagine them carrying on with their journey, but it was becoming harder to think it possible. She told Geavis about the past 48 hours. How she had taken a lonely train ride back to London where she faced an immediate problem: where could she go? Their house had been let, and to ask her son for hospitality seemed too embarrassing, given the terms on which they had last parted. So, she had wandered about, spending time in coffee shops and then at the police station, where she had insisted on staying all night. She was hungry for information and knew she would not sleep without it – so what was the point in booking into a hotel?

"Olivia," said Geavis. "I can't explain how I have ended up in this situation. But there is nothing to fear, I am sure about that. How *can* there be? I had an honest career, didn't I? I didn't do anything wrong."

"I hope you're right."

"It's just one of those things. I've got caught up in someone's political battle. But it will soon be over, and then we'll be off."

Geavis spent a little more time with Olivia than he had been led to expect. That seemed comforting, it made the police station seem a little less hostile.

Then he discovered why he had been allowed those extra minutes. The police had been completing the formalities of charging him. Once Olivia had been ushered away, this time to spend the night in a cheap hotel, he learned that he had been charged with three offences: false carbon accounting, climate change denial, and 12 sample counts of stealing the future of a child.

8

The climate camp grew continuously until the winter solstice. On that day, the camp staged a 'vigil of shame', when hundreds of protesters stood for five minutes' silent reflection on the ravages humans had wrought on the planet. Referring to the Christmas shoppers walking around the periphery of the square, Wilks said: "All those nice things: do you really need them? Is the destruction of life on Earth really a price worth paying for five minutes of fun before you discard all this junk? They may seem harmless luxuries now, but will you be feeling so smug when the tidal wave reaches your door, just as it reached my door, two months ago? It's absolutely clear: punish the Earth and be the Earth will punish us back in ways we will scarcely believe."

The event, which was live streamed, achieved higher viewing figures than any of the church services televised over Christmas. Some priests were envious – and admiring. "It was so Old Testament!" said one bishop, known for his conservative views. "Why can't we address our flocks with such hellfire from the pulpits? If I did so, the sky would fall in on me – and yet this lot get praised."

The vigil prompted a huge rise in membership of the Huddle for Love camp, which by New Year extended from Trafalgar Square to halfway down Whitehall. In the other direction it spread a little way along the Strand and up St Martin's Lane. A hard core of several hundred campers lived there all the time, but during the afternoons and evenings they were joined by thousands more for speeches, musical events and dance. It became a giant street party, one which began to smother much of the commercial life around it.

People who did not wish to take part in the protest began to avoid the area, while bands of Greenshirts from the camp challenged some of the shops and cafes over their commercial practices, accusing them of selling or serving products with an excessive environmental footprint. At first, establishments that provided food and drink to the protestors or allowed them to use the lavatories were spared criticism. But as the camp became more organised, the protesters successfully lobbied the government to provide mobile lavatories and several caravans carrying vegan kitchens, and the protesters' dependence on surrounding shops and cafes decreased. At that point, Greenshirts began actively to seek the closure of businesses they disapproved of.

The first to leave was a travel agent, found still to be selling holidays involving air travel. Protesters linked arms and blocked its doors; resistance was hopeless and it closed. Buoyed by that success, the activists took on a restaurant which had been found serving beef steak to regular and trusted customers. Greenshirts smothered themselves with fake blood and draped themselves over the tables to make the place resemble the scene of a massacre. Police cleared them once, only for the same to happen the following day, and the day after. The following week, its clientele driven away, the restaurant closed.

"Look," said Sarah Downwood in one of her regular meetings with the citizens' cabinet, "clearly you must be allowed to make your point, but you must also respect people's right to go about their business."

"Must we?" Firkin replied. "Even if their business is murder, or killing the planet?"

"At the very least, can you provide me with a list of the business practices you find unacceptable? We can look into legislation, but please, we need to regularise these protests, to bring them within the law. We can't just have anarchy."

To Firkin it seemed an odd thing to say: anarchy was surely a state where no-one had control. But in this case, there very much *were* people in charge: the Huddle for Love campaigners. Not only were they pulling the strings, they had weaselled their way formally into government. There was no point in their winning power if they were not going to use it. So they stepped up their harassment of local businesses, with the object of driving out every commercial outlet they deemed guilty of crimes against the climate.

Steadily, chain cafes began to give way to vegan co-ops, smart clothes shops to emporiums of loose-knitted shawls and vegan footwear. Pubs generally survived –if their beer won the seal of approval from the camp.

Only in one case did the Greenshirts meet their match. The owner of a pie shop in an alleyway to the north of Trafalgar Square refused to take it lying down when a dozen Greenshirts marched in, demanding to know what his pies were made of.

"Rats, squirrels and pigeons," he said quite brazenly, knowing it to be near the truth. The protesters lay down, obstructing the doorway. They smothered the pavement in front of his shop with red paint.

But what might have put off the clientele of a more refined restaurant did not put off the pie shop's customers, who took this as a badge of honour and assembled a mob of their own. They stepped over or onto the protesters' bodies, leading to scuffles. In one incident, an activist complained that someone had stepped on him with the words: "Get up, yer sod, or you'll end up in a pie yerself."

Supplies of meat, obtained in the countryside, were delivered at night by bands of burly guards. Somehow, the carrion would get through. The shop became a centre of counter-revolution, attracting from far and wide people who refused to accept the strictures of the Huddle for Love movement.

On Saturdays, Dave Bodger often turned up to give a speech. "Are we going to allow ourselves to be driven back to medieval poverty? The working man fought long and hard for the right to eat meat, and over my dead body are we going to give it up now!"

The Greenshirts withdrew – though were suspected of involvement a few months later when the pie shop owner was visited by officials from the Executive for Personal Carbon Budgeting. They claimed to have found irregularities in its accounts and succeeded in closing it down.

A week into January, the carnival atmosphere in the Huddle for Love camp began to fade. Temperatures plummeted and occupants of the camp were forced to act in accordance with its name. Even so, the frost was too much for many and they slumped off home.

"Global warming, my arse!" was a regular refrain outside the pie shop as its defenders stamped their feet in the snow to try to keep warm. The weather caused misery across London, and was blamed on the climate cataclysm: heating of the polar ice caps had caused cold air to slip southwards, officials claimed, displacing the jet stream and breaking the usual pattern of westerly winds.

Several deaths from hypothermia were now appearing on the daily total of deaths caused by the climate cataclysm. The power cuts returned, exacerbated this time by the decommissioning of some of the emergency generators, which had been keeping the lights on. This was all in accordance with the promise made to the protesters by the government.

Jake Raglan, lambasting the government for the loss of power, chose to overlook the fact that he had himself demanded the decommissioning of the generators. "This poor excuse for an administration has failed utterly to ensure that there is enough power for people to cook and keep warm," he said in the Commons, thumping the despatch box in his customary style. "Why has there been so little investment in green energy?"

What a cheek, thought Sarah Downwood as she rose to reply. The wind farms were there, the solar parks were there, but there just wasn't enough wind and sun to produce the power demanded. Hadn't Raglan badgered her to decommission the generators? But she felt unable to make this point, given that the final decision had been hers.

Instead, she resorted to blaming the extreme weather. "I am proud of what we have delivered on green energy," she said. "More wind farms, more solar farms than any other country. That is an achievement of which Britain can be thoroughly proud. But whatever contingency arrangements we have made, it has proved harder than we expected to keep up with extreme weather like that we are currently experiencing. We have to recognise that the climate cataclysm is advancing faster than any of us realised, and that we will suffer more extreme cold spells, as well as more extreme heat, in future."

The weather was not finished. The winds swung round from the north to the east and the cold intensified, with temperatures of minus seven being recorded in central London. For the first time, the daily toll of deaths attributed to the climate cataclysm topped 100, which made the leading headline on the evening's news bulletins. The protesters, still living in tents and unprepared for the cold, could take no more. Suddenly, even huddling together could not produce the warmth they required.

Wilks, Firkin and others walked to Downing Street and demanded to see the prime minister, who quickly reshuffled her appointments to make time.

"You have to do something – people are going to die here," said Wilks.

Downwood secretly wondered whether it would be entirely a bad thing if the climate camp was forced to disperse, but dared not suggest this. "Maybe you can appeal for blankets," she said feebly.

"This is not acceptable," said Wilks. "What we need is emergency shelter until the cold spell is over. You'll have blood on your hands if you don't provide it."

Downwood thought for a moment and said she would see what she could do.

A few hours later, at 10 in the evening, the doors of the National Gallery were opened and the protesters welcomed inside.

"What a gaff this is!" said Firkin as he wandered around, trying to choose his favoured quarters. After some deliberation he decided to doss down in front of *Christ Driving the Traders from the Temple* by El Greco, while Wilks preferred *Venus and Mars* by Botticelli.

*

A few miles away, in his cell at Highdown Prison, Bryan Geavis observed the weather with interest. This must be the coldest day for seven years, he thought as he kicked the powdery snow from his shoes in the exercise yard. High pressure was building over Scandinavia, drawing in freezing winds from Siberia. It was a familiar pattern, but not repeated every winter. He knew that once these winds set in, they could be quite persistent.

Geavis became so preoccupied with the cold spell that it distracted him from what he knew should be his main business: preparation for his forthcoming trial. It had been suggested to him that he should engage a lawyer, and he did get as far as having one visit him in jail: Michael Kowerd QC, one of London's leading defence barristers. But the fees seemed too high to Geavis, who had lost most of his pension when Albion Oil collapsed.

The government, which sometimes helped the victims of collapsed pension schemes, declined his request on the grounds that it could not be seen to subsidise people who had worked in the oil industry. Nor could he apply for legal aid – although his income was low, he was deemed to have sufficient resources to pay for his own defence because he still owned his house. But he was loath to sell it.

"I think you are being extremely unwise," the lawyer told him as Geavis announced that he had decided not to engage him and would instead represent himself. "This is an unknown, untested legal procedure and there will be a great number of people willing the prosecution to succeed. I will leave you my card in case you change your mind, and I urge you most strongly to do so."

Olivia visited Geavis several times, but each occasion was felt by both of them to be a disappointment. There seemed to be a growing distance between them, which neither could quite explain. Geavis was dazed by the situation he found himself in and what he considered to be the unfairness of it all; Olivia could not help thinking that he was holding something back, and might be guilty of some offence that he declined to discuss with her.

"Tell me please, once and for all, is there something you need to tell me?"

Geavis stared into space for a bit and then brought up the subject of the cold snap. Olivia knew him well enough to know that he didn't go on about the weather out of desire to make small talk – for him, it was what mattered. "If it falls by another 1.9 degrees it could be a January record in London," he told her excitedly. "But I don't suppose we'll quite get there. The chances are against it because average temperatures are half a Celsius higher than they were 50 years ago. It makes it just a little harder for a cold snap to nudge its way into the record books."

"Honestly," Olivia replied. "I know that is important to you, but you need to take your situation more seriously. I'm finding it so hard to get through to you."

Olivia now found herself torn between the affections of her husband and those her granddaughter. Adam and Chloe had taken Olivia in, reluctantly at first. But as she made an effort to spend time with Amber, and tried to get to the root of the girl's emotional problems, they began to appreciate her presence more. Adam and Chloe did as the psychologist instructed and encouraged Amber's participation in climate activism. They kept taking her to Trafalgar Square to join in the events there, but as far as they were concerned it wasn't helping her at all – on the contrary, she seemed to become more traumatised, crying out in her sleep. Olivia, thankfully, had more time to spend with Amber than they did.

"Tell me exactly what you were dreaming," she asked Amber after one especially broken night.

"I couldn't breathe. All the oxygen was gone," said Amber.

To Olivia, the girl needed distraction. She read her stories – tales that had nothing to do with her usual reading material, which generally related to suffering animals – and played games. Eventually, she began to tease out of Amber another anxiety: Amber was feeling jealous of her friend Misha, who seemed to be gaining all the attention.

"I want to be Misha," Amber told Olivia in the middle of one sleepless night. "If only I could be picked out like she is all the time. I care just as much, but no-one seems to notice me."

Misha certainly was being picked out. Virtually every week she was invited to Downing Street to take her place in the citizens' cabinet where Sarah Downwood, who would rather speak with her than with Wilks, Firkin or the other members, made sure she was granted full attention.

Misha had made several notable contributions. "Why don't we put health warnings on all food that isn't from the local area, telling people that it is damaging the climate?" she suggested in one meeting.

"What a brilliant idea," said Downwood.

Misha continued. "And why don't we add pictures of starving polar bears and burned kangaroos on the tins and packets, to make people feel guilty?" That suggestion made it into the next Climate Cataclysm Bill, in spite of officials' wariness.

"But you have to be aware, prime minister, that we can't feed the country without imported food," advised one of those officials.

"Just do it!" said Downwood. "Misha brings me such good ideas, and every time you try to stamp on them."

Between cabinet meetings, Misha was in constant demand from TV and radio studios, becoming joint chief spokesperson for the Huddle for Love camp. At first, Wilks had handled most of the interviews, but over time she preferred to put Misha forward simply because she knew that interviewers would deal much more softly with a 12-year-old girl.

During a particularly tricky period – when protesters from the camp were accused of prompting a market trader's heart attack by upending his cart when they discovered he was selling tomatoes flown part of the way from East Africa – Misha was sent to face the music. "I'm really sad about it," she said, when challenged. "But it's a fact that if we don't stop climate change, we're *all* going to die." The interviewer nodded and let it pass.

It was more or less inevitable that, when the courts service was looking around for someone to chair the new 'jury for the future', that Misha would be chosen. She was at first confused as to what it would entail, but after some basic training in legal principles she felt more confident about her role, even if she was still a little daunted by the responsibility.

At first, the government intended to have the jury instructed by a judge. But Wilks wasn't happy. "The low conviction rate for climate crimes is a disgrace," she told the prime minister. "It is quite clear that the existing legal system is inadequate to deal with matters of such seriousness."

Under pressure from the citizens' cabinet, the prime minister agreed that the newly established climate court would move to a fully inquisitorial system. There would be a panel of legal experts to advise the jury, but Misha and her co-jurors would be fully in charge. They would ask the questions, and they would make the final decisions.

As the date of the first, test trial approached, passions in the country began to run high. Queues formed outside the court's premises in the Strand. Much of the country seemed exercised by the case, with opinion divided as to whether the oil company executive, who had posed as a meteorologist and publicly denied climate change, deserved to be imprisoned or not.

"Deserves all he's going to get," said one man in a pub in Sidcup. "It's a conspiracy, isn't it? All these oil billionaires who've ruined the climate for their own self-enrichment. Disgusting, isn't it? He may not be Mr Big, but he's up to his neck in it, as far as I'm concerned."

His companion was not so sure. "Seems to be a bit harsh, to me.

Okay, what he said wasn't right, but it might have just been a slip of the tongue. Surely it wouldn't hurt us to show a bit of compassion towards the guy?"

And then there was the pie shop which, until it was closed down, had served as a seat of resistance for the dwindling band of mostly elderly people who did not believe climate change was happening at all. They had to be a bit careful and make sure that they did not speak too loudly, but for the moment the law against denying climate change only applied to things published or spoken in public; within the confines of a private space, the Pie Shop Deniers, as they came to be known, were free to say what they liked. Here, Bryan Geavis had become a folk hero.

"Stick a medal on him!" was one typical contribution to conversation in the weeks leading up to the opening of the trial. "He's the only one prepared to tell it as it is, isn't he?"

"That's right, mate," came the response. "There's dark forces in all this, isn't there? People who are making fortunes stopping us doing what we like. All those people putting up the wind turbines and the solar panels, they're alright, aren't they? And we have to put up with the poxy electricity which they produce, and get told we can't do this, can't do that."

Another chipped in. "And what for? There were just as many storms when I was a nipper as there are now, I swear. All this climate change stuff's been cooked up out of nothing."

Zoe Fluff, as ever, had her say, messaging her followers on Mob. "Still sobbing from trip to the Great Barrier Reef this morning. People who killed the coral must be brought to account. Fingers crossed for the right outcome in the climate court."

In the week before the trial, the social media site Mob put the case to a vote. Is Geavis guilty or not guilty? The government, the opposition, the court service and many others were outraged. Mob couldn't do that, they protested – it wasn't allowed publicly to comment on any current or imminent legal case. Still less could anyone try to pre-empt the verdict in a public poll. How could anyone make up their minds anyway, given that the evidence hadn't been presented?

Sitting in his chambers, Michael Kowerd, Geavis' would-be lawyer, thought privately that he would have demanded the case be dropped on the grounds that a fair trial was now impossible.

Mob was asked by the court to desist – or face prosecution itself. "Why should we take any notice of you?" replied its CEO, a safe distance away in California. "I don't come under your jurisdiction. And I'm not publishing anything, anyway. We're a network for private conversations – just bigger ones than you could have in a bar room."

In the end, he did relent – after negotiating with the government a tax cut for his company's British operations. As a result, the poll was never published, though there were rumours that it had come out more or less 50 percent in favour of Geavis' guilt and 50 percent against.

Come the day of the trial, however, and opinion began to slip away from Geavis, an important factor being the rising death toll attributed to the climate cataclysm. An interviewee on Diversity TV, who had expressed a little sympathy for Geavis, was silenced by Suza Shamon. "How on earth can you sympathise with him, when you can see just how many people these oil executives have killed?"

Shamon was ticked off for appearing to comment on a matter supposed to be sub judice, but it went no further.

Ignorant of all this fuss was Geavis himself, who had no access to Mob and who now tried to avoid all news. Nor did he have much to do with his fellow remand prisoners, mostly a collection of accused fraudsters and embezzlers.

He made one friend, Darren, who faced trial for falsifying the financial records of his energy company in order to win grants to which he was not entitled. They managed to have a few good conversations, in which they exchanged their personal stories along with the odd piece of dark humour. But conversation began to run dry when Geavis expressed his bewilderment at being charged. Geavis' perception was that Darren was guilty and knew he was guilty, while Geavis did not recognise his own guilt. That made them incompatible.

"Why do I have to be placed among criminals?" he asked Olivia during her last visit before his trial. "It's doing me no good at all. I'd rather read books in peace than speak to such people."

Soon after, at Olivia's request, the prison governor gave him several books on climate and meteorology, which kept him happier as his day of reckoning approached.

He kept asking himself: What do I have to do? Then: It is quite simple, surely? I just tell the truth and all will be well.

With one day to go, however, Geavis' confidence took a blow. He was informed by letter that he would be facing an extra charge: the manslaughter of 35 people in the Guy Fawkes Night storm.

Manslaughter, he said to himself over and over again, as if he couldn't believe the word had been applied to him. But I tried to help people!

9

On the morning of 1 March, Geavis was given an early breakfast and driven through south London to the new climate court in the Strand. He expected a bit of a crowd, but the extent of the commotion caught him unawares. As the van doors opened a huge cry went up and police struggled to keep the crowd back. The van was thumped and rocked. As Geavis was led out into the court building he noted that the protesters were five or six deep. His instinct was to estimate their number properly, though he had no time to do so. "Have they all come to see me?" he muttered beneath his breath, not knowing whether to be flattered or worried.

Once inside the court building, he was taken into a side room and the procedure was explained to him. The climate court would operate along different lines to traditional courts. The charges would be considered in order of seriousness. The first, false carbon accounting, did not worry Geavis unduly. Many people fell foul of that – it was so hard to understand how to fill in a carbon accounting form and so easy to forget everything you had bought. The worst he could expect for a first-time offence was a moderate fine. As for the climate change denial charge, he had expectations of being able to argue his way out of it. He had been back and forth over the words he remembered using in the Suza Shamon interview and believed that he had been misunderstood.

As for the other two charges – they really concerned him. He knew that he was a tiny cog in the workings of Albion Oil, but how could he deny that he had technically held the rank of senior manager? He might think it preposterous that he stood accused of the deaths of 35 people in a storm, yet the new law seemed to suggest he deserved a share of the blame. Could he challenge the fairness of the law itself? Could he argue that the manslaughter charge was excessive and that 'stealing the future of a child' was too vague a crime to mean anything? It seemed his only option.

At 10.30 he was called into a cavernous chamber with a long table at the far end. There were several cameras: owing to the importance of the case and the unprecedented interest in it, the proceedings would be live streamed.

Sitting in a central position was a girl he recognised as Misha from her many appearances on television. Flanking her on either side were half a dozen other children of varying ages, most of them older and larger than Misha herself. One of them, Geavis was taken aback to see, was Bunty.

The children were introduced to him as the jury of the future. To the left was another table of half a dozen men and women in gowns. These, it turned out, were legal advisers who were there to help the jury. To the right of the long table was a third table, occupied by another half dozen men and women, all in plain dress. This, it was explained to Geavis, was a body of specialists assembled to advise the jury on technical points of science. They had all been recruited, he learned, from an august body known as the National College of Expertise.

Geavis looked at them in turn and recognised four people. Bryony Smart, well known as a maker of documentaries on the natural world. And wasn't that Dr Aric Reissner, the anthropologist with whom he had appeared on *The Suza Shamon Show*? Guy Hovis, head of the Agency for Modelling Climate Chaos was there, too; Geavis nodded at him, though was not sure whether he would remember him from their earlier acquaintance. The other was Firkin, whom he recognised from the panel that rejected his application to become a climate influencer the year before. What is his expertise? Geavis asked himself. It turned out that Firkin had taken a PhD in the morality of capitalism, and it was thought that he could add some useful insights into the minds of oil company executives.

Misha asked Geavis to confirm his name and then read out the charges from a sheet of paper given to her by the lawyers.

"How do you wish to plead?" she asked after each one, and each time

Geavis said firmly, "Not guilty". Misha then consulted one of the lawyers on some small matter and the proceedings were underway.

The first charge turned out to relate to a couple of purchases Geavis had made for a barbecue the previous summer, which did not appear on his carbon return. It seemed trivial, a minor error, but Geavis could imagine why it had been brought: prosecutors in the climate crimes unit, worried that none of the other charges would hold, didn't want to go away empty handed; at least they would be able to pin *something* upon him.

"These were beetroot steaks, which I bought for a summer party," he said. "But I didn't consume them all: most were for my guests. So why should they go on my carbon return?"

But on whose carbon return *had* they been recorded? Geavis could remember who the guests were, but had he remembered to ask each of them to enter every steak they had consumed onto their own carbon return?

"It was a party nine months ago, and I simply don't have any recollection," he said. It seemed pointless to go on resisting; he was forced to concede that he had committed an administrative error and received a fine of £500. He was pleased to have it out of the way, as he thought it would allow him to save his energy for the more serious charges.

"You might want to take more care next time," said Misha.

Geavis nodded. He tried hard not to be irritated by being told off by a child young enough to be his granddaughter, but he couldn't stop himself. He thought of the grandeur of the courtroom, the solemnity of the legal process, the wigs and all that – and how it had been designed to intimidate the accused, to remind them of the gravity of the circumstances in which they found themselves. But nothing seemed quite as humiliating as having 12 children decide upon his future.

Next came the denial charge. "Mr Geavis," began Misha, referring to a script in front of her. "Are you aware that it is a criminal offence to cast doubt upon the fact that man-made climate change is raising temperatures and destroying the Earth?"

Geavis acknowledged that he knew this. Misha continued. "Then can I quote to you the words you used on *The Suza Shamon Show* last November? You told another guest on the programme: 'You speak with such great certainty about what is going to happen in decades' time, but then you swallow the Agency for Modelling Climate Chaos' claim that they couldn't see the storm coming hours ahead.' What did you mean by that? Because to me, it is like saying you don't think we *do* know what is going to happen to the climate in decades' time?"

"I was simply saying," said Geavis, "that there was no reason why the Agency for Modelling Climate Chaos should not have foreseen the storm coming. If they can tell what is going to happen to the climate in 100 years' time they ought to be able to forecast the weather in six hours' time."

"But that doesn't hold water. Because you were then asked: 'Are you questioning that we are headed for climate collapse?' and you replied, 'I don't know'. Why did you say you don't know? Everybody knows, surely? Or they ought to know."

"I was merely trying to get across my point. I didn't want the conversation to be diverted onto the climate when we were talking about a weather forecast."

"Then why didn't you say: 'Yes, I do realise that the world is heading for climate collapse?'"

"Does it have to be repeated at every opportunity?"

"If you are asked a straightforward question, I don't understand why you wouldn't answer it."

"To fail to say something, or to say you don't know something, is not the same as denying it."

Bunty, who had been listening studiously, then intervened. "But this fits a pattern of behaviour from you. As you know, I once came to your house to conduct a carbon assessment. I asked you: 'surely you want to tackle climate change, don't you?' And you didn't say a thing. What can we conclude from that, other than that you don't believe the dire emergency we're in – or that you don't care?"

"But that was a private conversation," said Geavis. "The denial law does not apply to private conservations. So why are you bringing it up?"

Geavis felt pleased that he had studied the law and seemed to know a bit more about it than Bunty did. Bunty was not sure about his answer and asked the table of lawyers for advice.

After a break of around five minutes she came back and said: "I'm told that you can't be charged for remarks you make in private, but that private conversations are allowed as character evidence. So there. It's what you said on the telly that's the criminal offence, but what you said to me is legitimate evidence of your denialism. On being asked whether we should be stopping climate change, you didn't say a thing. From that I take it that you refuse to accept the reality of the climate cataclysm. You are a denier."

"We've established that I didn't deny anything in public. Neither, for that matter, did I deny anything in the private conversation I had with you, Bunty. I failed to give you the answer you wanted, that is all."

"So, I'll ask you now, then," said Misha. "Do you accept that we are facing catastrophic climate change?"

Geavis took time to think. "I accept that temperatures have risen, because we can measure that. It is likely that the upward trend will continue in the near future."

"Just *likely*. Is that all?"

"We can't say *definitely* about things that haven't actually happened yet. We can only talk in probabilities."

"I don't understand," said Bunty, "why you can't accept established fact. If something has been deemed a fact, then it is true. You can't just say you don't know whether it's true or not. It *is* true. The science is settled."

"The problem we have is in mixing up observation with prediction. We can prove things if we can observe them by experimentation. But the trouble with the climate is that we can't carry out controlled experiments. We can't build two parallel Earths and subject one to one level of carbon emissions and the other to another. The best we can do is build mathematic models, but they are crude representations of the Earth's atmosphere, and we don't really know how accurate they are, because there may be factors we don't understand."

"What does that mean?"

"It means that temperatures could rise faster than we think, or slower than we think. There is uncertainty. But it offends me when I am told that the whole science is settled, because no-one should be saying that."

A boy of about 15, who Geavis later learned was called Sam, then spoke up. "It's you people who say you don't know about climate change who are the real problem. That's why nothing gets done and the world ends up on fire."

Another boy interjected. "And then all the animals die because we did nothing."

"What you need to establish," said Geavis, "is what scientific fact I am supposed to have denied."

"That the Earth's dying," said a girl at the edge of the table.

"What do you mean by *dying*? There seems to be plenty of life left on Earth to me."

"What about the dead trees and the fires, then? I know, because I've seen it on the telly."

Misha then spoke up. "Mr Geavis, you're not helping yourself, are you? We all know that the planet's dying."

There was then a brief interlude as a member of the group of experts went over to Misha and wrote out a little note for her. She read it and re-read it, and then told the courtroom: "These are the scientific facts as they are established in law, which cannot be challenged. The Earth has warmed by at least 1 Celsius above pre-industrial levels, and it is still rising, and will continue to rise at a rate of at least 0.1 Celsius per decade. It is permissible to suggest that temperatures are rising at a higher rate than that, but it is not permissible to say that they are rising at a lower rate. That is the law, as laid down in the Climate Change Denial Act, Mr Geavis, and we say you've broken it."

But not all members of the jury agreed. A boy called Morgan, who looked around 16 and whom Geavis would come to regard as a potential ally, then spoke up. "But if there is some uncertainty, doesn't that support what Mr Geavis has been telling us, that we can't be sure how much temperatures will rise in future?"

"But he doesn't think they'll rise at all," said Bunty.

"I didn't say that. I said they could rise by more than is currently predicted or less than currently predicted."

"So, you think they could rise by less than 0.1 Celsius per decade?" asked Misha.

"They could do. They have fallen sharply in the past on many occasions, without human intervention. Temperatures have always been naturally cyclical, and it is foolish to assume they will stop being so."

"But I just read out what it says in the Climate Change Denial Act and it says you're not allowed to say that temperatures are rising by less than 0.1 Celsius per decade."

"I didn't say they are definitely rising at less than that, I merely entertained the possibility. I also said they could rise by more than 0.1 Celsius per decade."

"And that would kill all the kangaroos," said Sam.

The proceedings went on in such fashion for some time. When the court was adjourned for lunch at 12.30, no-one felt they were going anywhere.

"Is this really going to work?" one lawyer asked the others. "More intervention this afternoon?"

Geavis was taken out and offered a sandwich, half of which he ate. When he was taken back to the court an hour later, everything seemed a little more organised. Misha had several sheets of paper in front of her, to which she referred regularly. But to open proceedings, she invited Firkin to the witness stand.

"I first met Mr Geavis in my role on the climate influencer interview board," he said. "On that occasion he said something which I think is very relevant to what he's been telling us today. He presented us with his weather records which we said he had recorded in his own garden. He claimed – and I took a note of this – that temperatures had *fallen* by 0.1 degrees in the past decade. Now what's that, if not denying established scientific fact?"

"Did you really say that?" asked Misha.

"Those were indeed the records which I have been taking in my garden for the past 40 years. And that's exactly what they say. Over the past decade temperatures have been on average 0.1 Celsius lower than they were the previous decade."

"But they can't be," said Sam.

"But that *is* what my thermometer was saying," said Geavis.

"It is in direct contradiction of what we have been told by the experts is established scientific fact," said Bunty. "Mr Geavis is telling us something that we know is untrue, and therefore the case is proven."

"But these are only the records from one place," said Geavis. "It doesn't mean that temperatures haven't been rising elsewhere. Globally, we have evidence to show that temperatures have risen by an average of 0.1 Celsius, but there is quite a variation between different locations, so the fact that they appear to have fallen a little in one part of south-eastern England is not inconsistent with the global average rise."

"So your garden just happens to be colder than anywhere else?" said Bunty. "It's just down the road from mine, and I know it's warmer than it used to be because we don't get snow anymore."

"But if he's saying that global temperatures have risen, he's not really denying it, is he?" said Morgan.

Firkin, who had been listening intently, with his arms folded, then continued. "I hadn't quite finished. It was my impression that Mr Geavis had simply made up these temperature figures that he claimed to have measured in his garden."

"Did you?" asked Misha.

"No, I did not," said Geavis. "That is a disgraceful attack on my professionalism. These temperatures were recorded on standardised equipment in the proper manner."

"Why do you say he made up the figures?" Misha asked Firkin.

"Surely, if your data is so out of line with the data being recorded by other people you should be asking yourself why," said Firkin. "And you should be correcting it. But Mr Geavis protested when we put this to him. It seemed to me that he was determined to put this false – and probably deliberately made-up – data into the public domain for one purpose alone: to try to deny climate change."

"Why didn't you correct the data?" asked Misha.

"This is outrageous," said Geavis. "My data was honestly collected. It would be completely dishonest to change it in some way because I felt it ought to be saying something different."

"What does the law say on this?" Misha then called across the table of lawyers and consulted with them for several minutes.

"The law says you cannot publish data in any form that is intended to mislead," she then said. "Or which purports to show that global temperatures are falling."

"And that is exactly what he was doing with his temperature records," said Bunty.

"How can anyone say temperatures aren't rising when the polar bears are drowning because the ice has all melted?" said Sam.

"If the law says temperatures ae rising by at least 0.1 Celsius a decade and you claim they've fallen it is as clear as anything that you have broken the law," said Bunty.

Geavis felt himself sinking. He held his head in his hands. How could you legislate the truth, he asked himself? But that is exactly what parliament had done. Whatever he said to defend his temperature records, to speak up for the integrity of scientific enquiry, it seemed merely to lead him deeper into the mire.

"There's another issue," said Misha. "On *The Suza Shamon Show* you refused to agree that the weather is becoming more unpredictable. Why did you do that?"

"Because I had seen the Guy Fawkes Night storm change direction and I successfully predicted that it would cross the Thames Estuary, even if the Agency for Modelling Climate Chaos did not."

Misha then turned to her table of legal experts again. "Are people allowed to say that the weather isn't getting more unpredictable?"

There followed another huddle, another mini conference, after which one of the lawyers announced: "The law is not clear on this. It doesn't specifically say anything about the predictability of the weather. But there is a general presumption that the climate is getting worse in every respect. So while there is no specific law against denying the weather is becoming less predictable, Mr Geavis could be said to have broken the spirit of the law. Now it is up to you people to decide whether that amounts to a criminal offence."

"I say it does," said Bunty.

"But did he actually say the weather isn't becoming less predictable?" said Morgan. "Or did he just fail to agree that that is the case?"

"Much the same thing, isn't it?" said Misha.

Soon after, the case was adjourned for the day. Thanks to the age of the jurors, it had been ruled inappropriate for them to be hearing a case for more than three hours a day. Geavis was frustrated because he sensed that things were going badly and desperately sought the opportunity to turn things around. There would now be 20 yawning hours before the case could resume. He knew he would be thinking about the case for all of that time, unable to move on. How could he distract himself? How could he sleep?

In the end, it wasn't just the legal case that kept him awake; it was hunger, too. That evening, back at the prison, he noticed that the supper portions were smaller than they had been on previous days. There was a problem with the suppliers, he learned, and it wasn't just prisoners who were finding food a little hard to come by. Over the preceding weeks, shoppers had found supermarket shelves emptying faster than usual, while prices had been rising steeply. Poor weather in southern Europe had interfered with the supply of fresh fruit and vegetables, it was reported. But it emerged there was more to it than that. Repeated power cuts over the winter had played havoc with heated greenhouses and also with the storage of food. Warehouses had been opened and all the food within them found to be spoiled. It had not been possible to make up for the lost stocks by bringing food from further afield, because transporting food directly into the country by air transport was now banned. It would take some weeks to put the shortfall right.

"It's shocking that this government cannot get on top of providing the basic necessities of life," Jake Raglan told the prime minister in the House of Commons. "You've sat idly by while this problem has developed, and now we have a fully-blown food crisis with millions unable to feed themselves properly."

Sarah Downwood had been fully briefed on the problems in the food supply chain, yet in her reply to the leader of the opposition she was loath to explain the full picture. To do so, she had been advised, could cause mass panic. There was already evidence of widespread hoarding, but what if she provoked looting and food riots? The only responsible thing, she felt, was to play down the crisis. Once again, as was her first instinct in these situations, she settled on blaming the weather.

"As the right honourable gentleman knows," she said, "we have had some very challenging weather recently, which has affected the supply of some foodstuffs. But I can assure the House – and the wider public, of course – that we are doing all we can to resolve the issues in a timely manner."

She failed to appreciate that she was handing Raglan his next line of attack.

"And you have known for years that the climate in Britain and across Europe was going to destroy agriculture. So why is the government, even now, failing to appreciate the seriousness of the climate cataclysm? It says so much about this prime minister that she didn't even mention the climate cataclysm in her answer. It is symptomatic of the devil-may-care attitude that has dogged her all along on this subject. The result of her inaction is that we face mass hunger. When, for the sake of the hungry people of this country, is it going to change?"

Downwood rifled through her mind for another climate change initiative with which to stave off Raglan's attack and impress the House. What else could she promise? She had tried everything, hadn't she?

Then she remembered the pledge she had made to Misha during the last meeting of the citizens' cabinet. "As the right honourable gentleman knows, we have the climate at the centre of all we do in this government. We have outlawed climate cataclysm denial. We have passed legislation in record quick time to help bring to justice those who have colluded with oil companies. The legislation is already bearing fruit, with the first trial underway. But today, I can announce a further measure. We will shortly be bringing proposals to parliament to force suppliers to put climate health warnings on all imported food, which will help to persuade consumers to buy local food and reduce the carbon footprint of everything we eat."

She sat down to cheers from some of her own MPs, sensing that she had turned a tricky situation into a triumph.

Only later, over a supper of halloumi and aubergine rissoles, did it start to bother her that her new law – while well-intentioned and perhaps helpful in the longer term –would do nothing to help a country in the midst of an acute food shortage. One option, which had been discussed with colleagues earlier, was to enlist the navy to help bring food to Britain from South

America, where harvests were good. But how could she do that when it would so clearly fly in the face of the legislation she had just announced in parliament, to put climate health warnings on all foreign food?

*

A few miles away in a jail cell, Geavis clutched his rumbling tummy and wondered whether he would get a half-decent breakfast before facing the second day of his trial.

And on the other side of London, Amber prepared anxiously for what she knew would be the biggest day of her life.

10

The next morning, Geavis had not long taken his seat in the courtroom when he was told there was a new witness to give evidence, this time from behind a screen. After some rearrangement of furniture, the witness was led in and invited to speak.

"Hi," said Misha. "Once you're settled, tell us exactly what you want to say."

There was a period of silence, and then a voice began. "It was something I was told by… what do I call him?"

"The accused," said one of the lawyers.

The voice from behind the screen was broken, trembling even. But even so, Geavis had no problem identifying the witness as Amber. What on earth was she doing there? What was she going to say?

There was another long pause, which Amber spent rehearsing over and over again the lines she had learned the day before. Then she said: "He told me that global temperatures were going to fall."

Geavis tried to think what she could have been referring to. He thought back to the time he and Olivia had walked to Amber's flat after the storm to check that the family was safe. He could remember it well. No, of course he hadn't said temperatures *were* going to fall, only that there was a chance they *could* fall; that it was within a wide range of possibilities. He tried to bite his tongue but found himself unable to hold back.

"That's a lie!" he said.

His comment was received with gulps from several of the children. Amber, though, was initially silent – until she began to cry, audibly.

"Don't be put off by that," said Misha. "You're doing really well. Take all the time you need."

Amber did take all the time she needed. Several times, a court clerk walked over to her with a pack of tissues. Geavis felt more and more wretched. What had he said? Amber was distorting the truth, that was for sure, but she might not be aware she was doing so. He knew he shouldn't have spoken to his granddaughter in public so sharply. Why couldn't he have left his response until she had left the courtroom?

Eventually, Amber spoke again. "He also told me that he was going to Brazil because people there live as they like and don't care about climate change."

This time, Geavis did bite his tongue. He knew he didn't want to raise his voice again, but what would he say even if he did? In any case, what Amber had said wasn't too different from what he really had said to her when he had visited her home shortly before his arrest. It was what he had felt at the time and what he still felt. He was fed up with falling living standards in Britain and he had wanted to leave because he thought life would be better in Brazil; that much was true.

"He said the Brazilians don't care, but did he say *he* didn't care?" asked Misha.

"He said they cheated on their carbon emissions in Brazil and he couldn't wait to get there," said Amber.

"Mr Geavis, did you say those things?"

"I can't remember my exact words," said Geavis. "But I may have said something about there being a different attitude towards climate change in Brazil. But of course I care. Everybody cares. I just got a bit carried away, I suppose. I was going to visit Brazil and I was excited by the thought of sun and a better climate."

"Sun? A better climate?" asked Misha. "What are you trying to say?"

"I like the sun. And the warmth. Doesn't everyone?"

"But that's what is killing the forests and wiping out the wildlife. How can you enjoy hot, sunny weather when you know it's killing the Earth?"

"That's unbelievable he said that," said Sam. "Sunny weather's not so much fun if you're a polar bear, is it?"

Geavis had nothing more to say. What was there to say, when there was such a gulf between him and the people in front of him? If they couldn't face a hot, sunny day without feeling guilty about it, there was little he could do.

Misha thanked Amber with a big smile. "That's all, thanks," she said. "But you should be really proud of yourself for what you've done today. You've really made a difference."

The rest of the jury clapped, then Amber was gone and the screen taken away.

There being no further witnesses, the jury of the future began to deliberate over the second charge: that Geavis had denied climate change. Members of the jury were given advice by the table of legal experts – on several occasions, Geavis noted, when the jury had not even asked for it. There was much toing and froing between the jury table and the lawyers' table. The children spoke for the most part in hushed tones, but even so, Geavis could make out much of what was being said.

"I say he's guilty," said Bunty. "No doubt about it."

Misha ignored her, as if to say that she thought it wrong to make such an assertion without first talking it out between themselves. "Tricky one," she said. "If we believe what the last witness told us, then he has definitely denied climate change. You are not allowed to say that temperatures are falling – we've been told that it's against the law. But if he didn't quite say what the witness told us he said, then it's a lot less clear."

"He just seems not to know," said Morgan. "Maybe he doesn't know so much about climate change as we do. Why should he? He didn't grow up with it. Must we punish him for having a poor education?"

"But you'd think he'd at least care," said Sam, "and he doesn't."

The jury was divided as to what Geavis had meant when he spoke on the television. The more they thought about it, the more ambiguous his remarks seemed to be. He could have been denying climate change, but then it could have been a slip of the tongue. Several on the jury accepted Geavis' argument that saying you don't know something is not the same thing as denying it. No-one was happy to go along with Bunty's suggestion that merely not answering her question was tantamount to denying climate change.

"He could just have been tired and not want to speak," said one of the younger children. "I'm like that, sometimes."

But all were agreed: the key to the whole thing was Geavis' conversation with the young girl who had just given evidence, and whom the lawyers had told them firmly that they must not name. If Geavis had really told her that temperatures were falling, then that was damning evidence that he was a denier.

"How do we know what she said was true or not?" said Sam. "It's not like your nose lights up when you tell a lie."

"She's not lying," said Misha. "She wouldn't lie. But then again, she might not have remembered the conversation properly. We've all done it."

"Why don't we ask the lawyers?" one of the other children said.

Misha summoned a lawyer, who suggested that it was up to them to decide whom to believe, and it was not for him to tell them. After a few more minutes' deliberation someone suggested they ask the table of experts instead. Might they be able to shed some light on the matter?

Firkin was more than happy to help.

"Research has shown," he said, "that female victims are more likely to tell the truth than are powerful males – the latter are used to having their way and have more to lose, and so will go to any length to fabricate a version of events which suits their case. The girl who has just given evidence is a victim because she is young and so will suffer much more from the climate cataclysm. Geavis is older, and he has all the power and privilege. Think about it." He winked at the jury as he retreated to the experts' table.

"That's interesting," said Misha. "So, although we don't know exactly what was said, it is more likely that the girl was telling the truth."

"That puts a different light on it," said Morgan.

"And he didn't show any concern at all when I mentioned polar bears," said Sam.

A few moments later the jury held a vote. The result was unanimous: Geavis was guilty of climate change denial. It was a serious charge, and he knew it would result in a heavy fine when he was eventually sentenced. But that would not be for a while. First, the two other charges levied against him would have to be heard. Although the jury had not done its full three

130

hours, the children's chaperone decided that they had had enough for the day and proceedings were adjourned.

The crowd outside the court was in jubilant mood. Geavis noted that it had increased in size compared with the day before. It was angrier, too, with many people shouting "Denier! Denier! Denier!" repeatedly.

Geavis was bundled into a van which then inched its way through the crowd. He felt strangely devoid of feeling as he was driven back to the prison. Had that really happened? It hardly seemed real. He tried to take an interest in the traffic instead and started counting the buses: 15 between Balham and Tooting Broadway.

Later on, however, he began to relive his experience in court, endlessly going over what he had said and what others had said. Surely, he could have made a better job of defending himself. But what should he have said? He couldn't think, not even after a couple of hours spent deliberating with himself.

After supper – as thin and mean as it had been the previous evening – his agonies were interrupted by a surprise visit from his wife. He was pleased that she had taken the trouble to come but was disturbed by the thunderous appearance of her face.

"Why on earth did you say that to her?" Olivia demanded. "Amber has been quite beside herself this afternoon. It was a disgusting thing to say to her when she has been feeling so low about the whole thing."

"But what else was I to say? Her words could convict me!" He looked down and began to study his hands, surprised to see that he was trembling. "Her words *have* convicted me."

"She's your granddaughter," said Olivia. "There was nothing personal in what she said. It wasn't her idea to give evidence in any case. She was talked into it and she did what she thought was expected of her. I have spent a lot of time with her over the past few weeks and I can tell you she is very sincere about what she believes in and what she says. What she doesn't need is you accusing her of being a liar."

"In any other situation I might agree with you. But I'm on serious charges."

"And you're making a fool of yourself."

"You know we can't afford a lawyer – the house will be gone."

"I told you not to go on that television programme and you wouldn't listen. Now look at what you've done!"

"I've got myself into this mess, I accept that. But at the very least I would hope for some support from you."

"Bryan, I helped lift Amber out of her depression and now – she's back where she was."

"But what about me?"

"I really can't take much more of your self-pity, Bryan, I really can't."

And with that, Olivia was gone, leaving Geavis sitting alone, stunned, depressed, until a prison officer took pity on him and suggested he might like some distraction. So, for half an hour before being locked back in his cell, he had a game of badminton with a murderer.

He lost.

*

A dozen or so miles away, Misha was having a good evening. The moment that she announced the verdict in court, the social media site Mob erupted in adulation.

"Got him!" read one much-shared comment. "Misha – you're a star!" Others concentrated on the next stage of the trial. "This is for Deptford," read one. "Now, let's send him down for life!"

Misha had been warned that she should not talk about the case outside the courtroom. She did, however, allow herself a smile and a wave as she left the building to cheers.

There would come a time when she would find the attention trying, when she wished for her old life back, when she yearned to be able to walk around unnoticed. But that time wasn't yet. She found it warmed her, to be a celebrity. One thought kept coming back to her: if the crowd is so pleased, it shows we have made the right decision. She wanted her moment in the limelight to last forever, and was disappointed when her mother and father tried to protect her from people who wanted to speak to her, shake her hand, clap her on the back.

"Can't we walk to the station?" she asked as she was shown into a taxi. No, she was told. The crowd might be friendly, but still she was in a potentially dangerous situation. She could be injured or crushed. And while the crowd seemed to be on her side, who could rule out the possibility that there was someone in the crowd who had disagreed with the verdict, who wanted to harm her?

The leaders of the Huddle for Love movement had set up a small committee to handle Misha's interests. They worried that she was tiring herself out by commuting to and from the eastern suburbs of London every evening and resolved to find her accommodation in the centre of the city. At this point, the Huddle for Love camp was still based in the National Gallery, but that institution's trustees were keen to have it moved out. Its presence was interfering with visitors, they complained. Worse, grease and steam from the vegan stews they were cooking in the galleries was threatening to damage the paintings.

Here was an opportunity, Evie Wilks suggested to Sarah Downwood, to formalise living arrangements for members of the citizens' cabinet. If the prime minister could have public-funded accommodation in Downing Street, why shouldn't members of the citizens' cabinet be provided with somewhere to live, too? It would be discriminatory not to offer them accommodation.

Downwood agreed, a little reluctantly, and asked officials to find a suite of rooms at a hotel in Piccadilly – though the citizens' cabinet also insisted on keeping one roped-off chamber at the National Gallery as a meeting room.

Misha moved into the hotel, too, with her parents.

There then arose the issue of how Misha should be conveyed safely on her daily journey to the climate court. To walk was impractical, given the size of the crowds that followed her whenever she appeared in public. Misha herself didn't like being taken by taxi. While all taxis were now fully electric, to her they still looked too much like the evil petrol and diesel vehicles of recent history, which, she had been told, killed millions of people with their toxic fumes. She demanded a purer form of transport. A solution arose during negotiations with gallery staff, who had connections with other collections around the city. The following morning, an old sedan chair was brought over from the Museum of National Shame (formerly the Victoria and Albert Museum) and Misha was taken to the court in that.

By now, millions were watching the daily live streaming of the court case, and everyone seemed to have an opinion. On Mob, and amongst the crowd outside the climate court, there was a clear bias towards people who believed Geavis was guilty. In private conversations at work, in pubs and at home, opinion was more mixed. One man, interviewed on a local radio station in the north, spoke for many when he said: "It could happen to any of us, couldn't it? That's the trouble: a few loose words, a bit of misunderstanding and you're nicked."

But opinions seemed to be hardening by the day. The opening of Geavis' trial happened to coincide with the first occasion that the official death daily toll from the climate cataclysm hit 200. As usual, there were some questions about how this total was being calculated, with a few people in government arguing that it was unreasonable to include every elderly person who had died of respiratory illness, especially considering, if anything, that the toll had tended to diminish with warmer winters. But out in the country this was a minority view. The death toll was beginning to resemble an epidemic, suggested a commentator on *The Progressive*, which meant that the government and society at large had precious little time to act before a tidal wave of deaths swept over the country. It was a prospect that terrified many, and which expressed itself in increasingly intolerance of anyone considered to be indulging in unnecessary luxury. In Sidcup, a woman had her windows smashed for leaving her lights on beyond what neighbours decided was a reasonable hour. In Harpenden, a family had their barbecue overturned, causing them to suffer burns. "That's producing methane!" their assailant shouted. "That's 25 times as potent as carbon dioxide!"

What public sympathy remained for Geavis began to wane on the third morning of his trial. Many could relate to the narrative of a man who had fallen foul of the climate denial law thanks to a few loose words; fewer were sympathetic to a man who, they believed, had sought to hide the fact that he had been a senior executive of an oil company. This was the crux of the third charge on which Geavis was standing trial: stealing the future of a child.

He soon found himself struggling.

"Mr Geavis, can you explain exactly what position you held at Albion Oil?" asked Misha.

"I spent most of my career as a meteorologist," he said.

"And why would an oil company want a meteorologist? To spread lies about the climate?"

"Not at all. It was dangerous work on the oil rigs. It was my job to produce a weather forecast to tell the managers whether it would be safe to work outdoors or not."

"Did you ever ask yourself about the morality of you work?"

"My job was simply to keep people safe. I was a small cog in this organisation. It wasn't my business to make judgements as to whether the world should be burning oil."

"So, whose business was it to ask that question?"

"I don't know. Not mine. I just had to forecast the weather."

"Don't you think you should have asked yourself what you were doing and who you were serving?"

Geavis was in a quandary. It would be easier, for sure, for him to denounce the company for which he had worked, to agree with the jury that oil was an evil industry but to downplay his personal role in it. But no, he wasn't going to do that. His integrity would not allow him to.

"I accept that from the point of view of today it might seem wrong to have been drilling for oil," he said. "But that is not how it felt at the time. When I started work, this was not seen as an immoral industry, and those of us who worked for it were not seen as criminals. We were providing the energy which kept people warm, which helped put food on the table. Maybe we should have worked harder to find a different form of energy, but at the time burning oil was the only choice we had. It was seen by almost everyone as perfectly acceptable."

"Acceptable?" asked Bunty. "How can you say that? How *dare* you say that?"

"If you go back 200 years, most people were poor," said Geavis.

"Pathetically poor. They were hungry. Infectious diseases were rife. People died much younger than they do today. Then we grew richer. Our health improved. We had enough to eat. It was all thanks to industrialisation, where human labour was replaced by machine. And what was it that made the difference? It was all down to one thing: cheap energy. First it was coal, then oil. Yet people now can't seem to see that so much of what they take for granted was down to these fuels."

"Is this true?" Misha asked the table of experts.

There followed a conference, in which Dr Reissner was seen to take an especially prominent role. The idea that people were much poorer 200 years ago was a myth, he explained. There were no statistics on poverty going back that far, so how could anyone possibly claim with confidence that people were poorer then? What was for sure was that they lived closer to nature, that they had better access to land. They didn't suffer from the anxieties that people do today. They weren't poisoned by fumes created by the burning of fossil fuel. And they didn't live in fear of climate breakdown and total environmental collapse. It was plain that what had caused poverty was industrial capitalism, driven by fossil fuels.

Misha listened intently. "The facts are that no, people were not poorer in the past than they are now, so your point is invalid," she then told Geavis.

"You say people are not richer than they were two centuries ago? But that is absurd," said Geavis.

"Please do not try to make that point again. It has been ruled to be untrue."

"It just shows how right we were to find him guilty of climate cataclysm denial," said Bunty. "He clearly has a problem accepting the truth."

"But this cannot stand!" said Geavis, becoming quite red. "It is plain to anyone who studies the past that humans are healthier and better fed than they were prior to the industrial revolution. I cannot and I will not accept what you have been told."

Misha was thrown by his intervention and did not know how to handle it. Hadn't Geavis just been told that burning fossil fuels had caused mass poverty around the world? So why was he so persistent? Here was a man, who had already been found guilty of climate cataclysm denial, who was making things worse for himself by being so stubborn. It didn't seem to make sense. It was embarrassing.

She glanced over to the table of lawyers for support. One of the lawyers stood up and explained for the benefit of Geavis and the jury. "For the purposes of the climate court, once a fact has been established by the National College of Expertise, that is it. It cannot be challenged. Indeed, any opinion that runs counter to it must not be mentioned again."

"Exactly as I thought," said Misha. "Can we please now move on?"

Geavis slumped in his chair. He could see no way forward, and he couldn't explain why. Had he been made complacent, he asked himself, by the youthfulness of the jury? Had he underestimated them? That couldn't be it. He knew far more than they did about weather and climate, surely, and he thought he knew more about the law, too. Yet somehow, he found himself in a legal process which was crushing him, and there seemed no-one he could talk to, no-one whom he could ask advice and, since Olivia had turned against him, no-one who could console him.

The jury moved on to the question of Geavis' role at Albion Oil. He had explained his role as a meteorologist, but attention now turned to the last five years of his career; years that were potentially more damaging to his case.

"Can you explain your exact role during this time?" asked Misha.

"Yes," said Geavis. "There came a point when Albion Oil's operations in the North Sea were declining. The company no longer had so many people working on the platforms and, consequently, it didn't need so many weather forecasters. My job was abolished. I could have left the company at that time, but it was difficult for me. I was a little too old to start another career but a little too young to retire. So I took a transfer within the company. I was offered a role in the public relations team. My particular job was to publicise Albion Oil's environmental projects. There was a site down by the Thames which had been occupied by an oil refinery and which the company was obliged to return to marshland, as it had once been. The apparatus was taken away, the land meticulously cleaned and the sea wall breached to allow it to flood at high tide. The place was given a pleasantly naturalistic name – the Broad Washes – and became quite an impressive nature reserve for wading birds. That is what I helped to publicise."

There followed some deliberations between the jury and the table of lawyers, at the end of which Misha read aloud from a piece of paper, which had been handed to her. "But what you told people about this project was less than truthful, wasn't it? I refer to the time you told journalists that eight pairs of dark-bellied Brent geese had become established on the marshes. In fact, by this time you knew that one of those pairs was already dead, having been snared by some discarded plastic piping which you had failed to remove from the site. Isn't that true?"

Geavis remembered the case well. "Yes, it was an embarrassment," he said. "But I didn't know that the birds were dead at the point I put out the press release. There was a failure of communication. But of course, when the dead birds were spotted by reporters who were being given a tour of the site it caused a great hoo-ha."

"Hoo-ha? It was a crime."

"It was an accident."

"It was an act of criminal negligence."

"It was only two birds. After that, the piping, which somehow had been missed during the clear-up of the land, was removed and the colony became very well established."

"*Only* two birds! You write them off as if their lives meant nothing. The poor creatures!"

Bunty had become quite excited by this. "So once again you were caught out telling lies," she said.

"But if he didn't mean to kill the birds…" said Morgan.

"Hardly makes a difference," said Bunty. "The company lured the birds to their deaths. It presented them with what looked like a suitable habitat but one which was in fact ridden by junk from an old oil refinery. What's the practical difference between that and deliberately trapping or shooting birds for your own perverse entertainment?"

"We increased the numbers of birds in the Thames Estuary," said Geavis. "It was a thought a great success at the time."

Misha had another word with one of the lawyers, who presented her with another note from which she read. "But wasn't the truth of it that the whole point of this nature reserve was to launder your company's reputation in order to try to justify or excuse the huge damage that it was doing to the planet by producing oil?"

"You could argue that, I suppose. There was an expression at the time for what you describe – 'greenwashing' – which meant trying to establish environmental credentials in order to distract from less environmentally-friendly operations. But I think that is too cynical. We did establish bird colonies and I was proud of them."

"But presumably the birds would have been there anyway if you hadn't built your oil refinery in the first place," said Morgan. "At best you put right a little bit of the damage you had caused."

"Perhaps that is true. But as far as my involvement was concerned, we started with poisoned land, we cleared it up and returned it to nature."

"While still producing and burning oil elsewhere," said Misha.

"And killing birds with plastic pipes," said Sam

The jury spent some time discussing the issue before Misha announced: "We have established that – in your own words – this nature reserve was just a bit of greenwashing for the evil oil business of oil production in which your company was involved. But what we really need to know is how senior your position was at Albion Oil." She produced another note. "You told police after your arrest that you were a member of senior management."

"I was given a senior management title, yes," said Geavis. "But it was only a title. It was just to make me feel a bit better for having my old job as a meteorologist taken away from me, that's all. I wasn't making the big decisions. I wasn't involved in oil production."

"But a senior management position is a senior management position," said Misha.

"In name only. No decision that I made led to a single extra barrel of oil being produced. It really didn't."

"Thank you, Mr Geavis. We have all we need."

The jury went into a huddle once again and members conferred amongst themselves. Geavis could make out a few words of what they were saying, but he hardly needed to. Their body language and constant nodding said it all. Within 20 minutes they had all gone back to their seats and Misha was announcing to the court: "Mr Geavis, we find you guilty on 12 counts of stealing the future of a child, by virtue of you being a senior executive at Albion Oil."

Sentencing was to be deferred until the end of the trial, but Geavis knew what it meant: he was now facing a jail sentence of up to 10 years – a period that would bring him close to the end of his natural lifespan. As the news was relayed to him, he collapsed in his chair, leading a court clerk to fear for his health; she came across to check that he was still conscious. He was, but was too preoccupied with his own misery to do more than to acknowledge that he had not passed out and to wave her away with his hand.

The wretchedness of his situation had overcome him. Why had he and Olivia left it so long to attempt their move to Brazil? Had they left days earlier they would be there by now, splashing in the sea, enjoying barbecues at sunset. Now, there was no hope of ever leading that life. All that stretched ahead were long years in prison – and perhaps the hope of a few twilight years as a free man, if his health held out.

But there was worse to come. Tomorrow, he would face a more serious charge still: the manslaughter of 35 people in the Guy Fawkes Night storm.

I tried to save people, he told himself. I could have been the hero of the hour. Instead, I am going to be blamed for it – blamed for a storm that no man could have started.

For Misha, it was a triumphal sedan chair-ride back to her hotel. Huge cheers went up whenever she turned a corner into a new street, with just one or two dissenting comments, expressed in whispers.

"Does she look to you like someone who's just had her future stolen from her?" said one man to his friend, drawing glowers from a woman beside them.

Misha waved and smiled at the crowds. What joy it felt – though at the back of her mind was an uncomfortable thought: that she was beginning to live in a bubble. Would the adulation ever become too much?

She was still thinking this when, on the way out of the north-western corner of Trafalgar Square, an incident changed her mood completely.

She first became aware of chanting. Then, out of the corner of her eye she noticed a section of the crowd surging towards her, with some people being thrown to the ground by its force. She had hardly registered that,

140

though, when the window of her sedan chair was shattered, showering her with glass.

She screamed and screamed, as the four bearers of her chair accelerated from a walk to a run. A few minutes later she was safe, stretched out on the vast, softly sprung bed in her fourth-floor hotel room, recovering her breath. But it was the best part of an hour before she felt able to speak again.

"Mummy, what happened?" she asked.

11

Although you wouldn't have guessed it from the trolley of food delivered to Misha's room that evening – piled high with salads, falafel, couscous and even a little meat and fish which she consumed without thinking, and later felt guilty about – the food shortages elsewhere in London were becoming critical. In some of the poorer boroughs, supermarkets were closing and barricading their doors, so little food was there on the shelves. Most people still managed to eat, but only thanks to a black market in which staple foods were selling for many times their normal prices. In places, rioting had broken out – including in a few of the streets around Trafalgar Square where Misha's sedan chair had been attacked.

The emerging leader of the protests, Dave Bodger, denied that the attack on Misha's sedan chair had been planned by a group of Pie Shop Deniers.

"No, no. That's not us at all," he told reporters. "I didn't sanction it and I don't think it's right. She's only a girl, after all." But to many ears he had stopped a little short of condemning the action, which cost his movement much sympathy.

"They're just a bunch of louts – privileged, angry white males lashing out in frustration that they're not the top dogs anymore," wrote a columnist in liberal newspaper *The Progressive*. "They can't bring themselves to accept the evidence that it is the climate cataclysm that has brought us these food shortages, and so they try to create demons. Misha, who has set an example to us all by facing up to the realities of the cataclysm, is just a convenient punchbag to help them release their anger."

While the identity of the stone-thrower was never uncovered, the supposition that it was one of Dave Bodger's crowd was enough for Evie Wilks to demand that the roofer-turned-would-be-revolutionary be arrested.

"You've got to neutralise the hate-mongers," she told Sarah Downwood at the following day's meeting of the citizens' cabinet. "Or there'll be merry hell from us."

Downwood apologised, but said that she could not order anyone's arrest. "I share your concern but it's a matter for the police and the courts," she said. After seeing Wilks' expression she added: "And I'm sure that the police will be doing everything they can to bring the perpetrators of violence to justice. It is, of course, possible that we could remind them of their duties."

The food shortages dominated Downwood's daily round of meetings. Was it true that the climate could be blamed for the food shortages? Or if not, what was to blame?

Ministers looked at a paper written by an agronomist at a university in the Midlands. Last year's harvest had been exceptionally light, he revealed, down 15 percent on the year before. Why, it wasn't easy to tell but he speculated that it might have something to do with what he called the "extreme averageness" of the weather over the previous summer. It is normal, he argued, for the British summer to go through dry periods and wet periods, warm periods and cold periods. Yet last year, he noted, temperatures had remained more or less constant throughout the season. Rainfall, too, had been remarkably evenly spread throughout the summer months. Might this, he wondered, have interfered with the normal development of crops? He wasn't sure, and more work would be required, but he felt it was certainly a worthwhile line of enquiry. And with the climate cataclysm, could it mean more such summers, where crops would be deprived of the stimulation caused by sharp changes of weather?

Extreme averageness was not a concept any members of the cabinet – the official cabinet, that is – had heard about, but they didn't feel qualified to dismiss it.

"Maybe there is something in it," one minister said. "And if that is going to become a normal British summer in future then we are going to have a problem."

Yet, a group representing farmers told a different story. The reason the

143

harvest had been so light, they argued, was that they had struggled to get the right machinery at the right time. It was legal to buy limited amounts of diesel fuel for the purposes of farm machinery, but it required a permit, and there had been a delay in issuing permits, with the result that tractors and harvesters sat idle. Moreover, the new electric tractors in which some farms had invested were struggling to do the work of their diesel-powered predecessors. They took too long to recharge and didn't seem to hold their charge as long as their manufacturers claimed they ought to. With the harvest delayed, some crops had been left to rot in the ground.

The cabinet was agreed. The permit system for agricultural equipment would have to be improved. They discussed and settled on a plan to issue an extra round of permits – for one trial season only. To make up for it, to try to soak up the extra carbon dioxide which would be emitted on farms, farmers would be obliged to plant a tree for every extra litre of fuel they burned.

The trouble was that, under the agreement Downwood had reached with Evie Wilks, any policy connected with climate change or fossil fuels first had to be approved by the citizens' cabinet. And when Sarah Downwood put the plans to it, its members were firmly opposed.

"Absolutely no bloody way," Wilks told her. "Carbon emissions go in one direction only – and that's down."

"But this would only be a temporary measure, offset by tree planting," said Downwood.

"I wasn't born yesterday. 'Just a little extra fuel,' you say. Oh, yeah – and then they'll want more. No bloody way! We all know why the harvests are falling – because the climate apocalypse is destroying the crops. And it's only going to get worse so long as we keep messing up the climate. We are not going to accept any relaxation of this diesel permit system. Quite the reverse: we demand it is phased out – or we'll bring down the government."

Downwood prepared herself for a rough ride in the Commons and she wasn't disappointed. Jake Raglan had his tail up.

"Why are there people hungry on British streets? Why are the harvests producing less each year? It is because this government still does not understand the urgency of the climate cataclysm. Eliminate those emissions

144

and we can start growing food to feed everyone again. I say to the right honourable lady: do something right now, or face going down in history as the bringer of famine to our country."

Downwood struggled to make herself heard above the opposition's cheers; many of her own MPs wondered whether she was up to the task.

"The honourable gentleman does a disservice to those of us on this side of the House," she said. "We are well aware of the damage that the climate is doing to agriculture. We know the challenges we face as British summers go through lengthy periods of extreme averageness. And we are on top of it. Today, I can announce that we will be bringing forward that day that we arrive at zero emissions by the phasing out agricultural diesel allowances. Instead, we will be introducing financial incentives for farms which are run on a collective basis and which do much of their work by hand. I have one further announcement to make. The gentleman talks of the climate cataclysm. This government is one step ahead in realising the seriousness of the situation. In recognition of the food crisis, from today we are renaming the Department for the Climate Cataclysm. It is now the Department for the Climate Apocalypse. It's all hot air on his side of the House. On our side, it is real action."

For the moment, Downwood had succeeded in staving off political disaster, but there were to be consequences. Following that day's exchanges in the Commons, eight in ten members of the public believed that the food shortages had been caused by the climate apocalypse and rejected the farmers' explanation. Some rural communities acted to prevent food leaving their districts, erecting barricades to prevent lorries taking crops away. With shops empty, hungry people from the towns were beginning to travel to rural areas to see what they could find – to see whether they could buy direct from the farmers, or to steal. In many places they were chased away. In Kent, a group of vigilantes stopped every vehicle, every bicycle and told outsiders to turn around and go back where they came from.

"It is our village, our food!" they told them. "Go back and eat your own food, scum!"

*

The atmosphere in Highdown Prison was becoming heated. Portion sizes at supper had fallen to less than what inmates felt they had a right to expect. A furious stand-off with catering staff erupted into a serious disturbance, with canteen tables overturned and chairs thrown at fleeing officers. The inmates refused to move until they were offered more to eat – which eventually they were, after a nearby supermarket agreed to release some of its rapidly-diminishing stocks upon pleas from the prison governor.

It was a distraction Geavis could have done without, as he prepared himself for the most serious stage of his trial. How was he going to defend himself against a manslaughter charge?

To him, the whole business seemed to be nonsense. Of course he hadn't caused the Guy Fawkes Night storm. No individual could cause a storm – the charge assumed he had supernatural powers. And even if it could be argued that the storm had been the product of carbon emissions from fossil fuels, he could hardly take the full blame – his role had been infinitesimally small.

He had seen enough of the climate court to know he could no longer count on common sense prevailing. But what option was there other than to argue his position clearly and logically? He tried to imagine how Michael Kowerd, the lawyer he had refused to employ on the grounds of cost, would have approached his defence. Surely he, too, would have argued against the absurd concept of blaming a single person for creating a storm. He would have come armed with facts about how this storm was not unique, and how such events had happened since before human history. Yes, that is what he would have done. Fortunately, Geavis already held many of those facts in his head.

The prison was calmer the following morning, when Geavis was driven away; the inmates were sleeping off their exertions and a fine meal, which had eventually been prepared for them. Geavis felt placid, too, as he was taken through south London. The crowds outside the climate court seemed more orderly; after the previous day's incident in Trafalgar Square, the police presence had been strengthened.

As for Misha, her sedan chair was accompanied all the way from Piccadilly to the Strand by a convoy of six armoured vehicles.

Proceedings got off to a slow start, with constant interruption as the lawyers took their time to brief Misha and other members of the jury. Pieces of paper passed back and forth, and at times the table of experts was consulted, too.

"Good morning, Mr Geavis," Misha eventually began, long after the scheduled start of 10.30. "I have to tell you that new evidence has come to light and that as a result you have now been charged with a further offence of ecocide – for causing the deaths of a colony of birds in the Thames Estuary. Do you understand the charge?"

"I'm not sure I do, no," said Geavis.

"It has been discovered that a large number of seabirds were killed on the night of the storm and in the subsequent weeks as a result of the destruction of their nesting sites by the high water and waves. Do you now understand?"

Geavis found himself unable to reply. Could this business get any worse? The manslaughter charge was bad enough, but ecocide, he had learned, would be treated by the climate court as equivalent to murder. Should he be convicted, he would face a life sentence.

"Do you understand?" repeated Misha.

"I understand the charge itself. As to why I find myself accused of it… that will take a little longer to comprehend."

After a break for a few more minutes of conferring, Misha addressed Geavis again:

"I want to ask you a few questions about your time at Albion Oil. At what stage of your career did you first hear about climate change?"

"I was aware, at the time I was studying meteorology, there was a theory that human activity would warm the planet. The theory had been around for 100 years, in fact – although when I started out in the business, people seemed to be more worried about the prospect of another ice age."

"So, if you were aware of climate change, why did you start working for an oil company? Surely you knew what damage you would be doing."

"I had no reason to feel ashamed of what I was doing. It was a useful public service."

"Public service? But you were destroying the planet!"

"That is a little far-fetched. I was only giving weather forecasts."

"But you were serving Albion oil. You can't get away from that."

"And Albion Oil was providing a product that was essential to maintain living standards. It wasn't as if the company was burning all the oil itself; it was extracting it from the ground for everyone to burn – in their homes, in their cars, for all manner of purposes. If burning fossil fuels is a crime, it is one in which we are all implicated."

"No. Not my generation. We don't have our fingers in it. But we are the ones who will suffer from what you did, who have had their futures taken away."

"You do not even realise how you have benefitted from the oil industry. You have been brought up warm and well fed, haven't you? You've been brought up in a world that is almost free from hunger and pestilence?"

"Mr Geavis, we've been here before. You are not allowed to say that people are better off now than they were before the fossil fuel age began, because it has been ruled not to be a fact."

Geavis put his head in his hands. He knew he was being led in a direction that he did not want to go, yet he could not stop himself. He was being goaded, made to sound harsh, and he knew it was doing his case no good. But he knew how much it would hurt to concede a point that he felt was fundamentally wrong. As he struggled with this, Misha went on.

"Do you even accept the connection between the emissions from the oil you were helping to get out of the ground and the fatal storm of last November?"

Geavis thought for a moment. What if he said yes? Would it help him? He guessed not. He would then be all but admitting that Albion Oil – and by implication himself, too – bore some responsibility for the storm, however small. No, he would have to say what he really thought.

"There is a fundamental problem with blaming the Guy Fawkes Night storm on man-made changes to climate. Evidence from tide gauges in the Thames Estuary suggests that while average tide levels have risen by 15 centimetres over the past 70 years, there has been no upward trend in the maximum level of tidal surge in all that time."

"That doesn't sound right," said Misha. "How come London flooded, then? Places don't just flood, not without climate change."

"But they do."

"It's incredible. You're still denying the climate apocalypse, even though you've just been found guilty of it."

"What happened last Guy Fawkes Night was far from unprecedented. If you look back through the records, this storm was not as bad as those in 1987, 1953 or 1703, when 8,000 people were killed and 100 ships wrecked. It was a type of storm that is liable to happen by chance, and indeed *has* happened by chance on many occasions."

"I think we'll see what the experts think of that."

The experts seemed to take an age to decide, and were unusually divided. Firkin was seen to shake his head several times as Guy Hovis took a lead and expounded his own view. Eventually, Hovis stood up and delivered his verdict.

"While it is technically true that we have not yet been able to show an upwards trend in tidal surge heights in the Thames Estuary, the data is problematic because it is so at odds with the general narrative of the climate cataclysm. I feel it is not right. Therefore, the data must be disregarded while we await a better means of measuring tidal surge heights".

"But that is ridiculous!" said Geavis, earning him a rebuke from Misha for his interruption. When he was quiet again, Hovis went on.

"The reference to the alleged storm of 1703 cannot be allowed. There are no reliable records which prove that a severe storm took place in that year."

"But there *are*," said Geavis. "There are numerous witness reports, and evidence of damage, such as several hundred fallen chimney stacks, which are consistent with winds of 100 miles per hour, or more. That is far more severe than what we suffered last November."

Misha consulted with the experts again, and then continued. "It is not a fact that winds of more than 100 miles per hour were measured, and you must not repeat that claim."

"But it is in the records! It has been quoted as fact for as long as I can remember."

"It has been discontinued as a fact," said Hovis.

"Why? You can't decide a fact is no longer a fact because it does not suit you to believe it."

Misha was handed another piece of paper. "Many of the accounts of this storm can be traced to Daniel Defoe, who was not a scientist but a writer of fantasy. It is now considered that he exaggerated everything.

Furthermore, official records, such as they exist, may have been fabricated by the Admiralty in order to save itself from the embarrassment of losing 100 ships due to their incompetent captains."

"To lose them all on one night!" said Geavis. "That signifies a very great meteorological disaster. It cannot have been otherwise."

"Mr Geavis, the storm which you claim happened is not a fact, and that is that."

Geavis shook his head in defeat, and just wished the whole business over, no matter how many years he would have to spend in jail. Even the prison regime of being locked in a cell for many hours a day, could surely not be as bad as the humiliation to which he was being subjected. But just as he thought things could not get any worse, Misha's words, for the first time in many hours in the court, seemed to offer him a glimmer of hope.

"The facts are as follows: the Guy Fawkes Night storm cannot be attributed wholly to the climate apocalypse, as it could, just possibly, have happened by chance. But the climate apocalypse greatly increased the risk of the storm happening. Therefore, on the balance of probabilities, Albion Oil may be held responsible – even if we cannot be absolutely sure."

The opinion Misha read out seemed to confuse her as well as her fellow jurors, who now sought to discuss what they had heard. From what he caught of their conversation it seemed to Geavis they had expected certainty and had been given something a little less.

"How can we convict him for something if we can't be absolutely sure that he's responsible?" said Morgan.

"But if it's overwhelmingly likely, isn't that good enough?" said Bunty.

"I think we have to be certain, and we can't be."

"It's okay to have reasonable doubt, isn't it?" said a voice from down the table.

"No, it's not," said Morgan. "It's got to be *beyond* all reasonable doubt."

"What does that mean?"

"It means we've got to be absolutely certain."

"Not absolutely," came another voice. "But pretty well certain."

"More or less certain," somebody offered.

"Ninety-nine percent sure," suggested Misha.

"Ninety-nine point nine nine nine nine nine nine," said Sam.

The deliberations went on and on until the chaperone called it a day. She worried the decision was beginning to hurt the children's heads. They couldn't be allowed to become stressed by the task that was being asked of them. They would have to be sent away to sleep on it, and to come back in the morning – or rather Monday morning, given that the court would not be sitting over the weekend.

On his way back to the prison, Geavis mulled over a thought which had occurred to him during the jury's seemingly endless deliberations. Should he, after all, give Michael Kowerd a call and hire him for the remainder of the case?

Why was I so quick to dismiss him? he asked himself, over and over again. Kowerd would have known what he was doing. Things certainly couldn't have turned out worse. Was there any chance, even at this late stage, that Kowerd could get him off the last two charges, and possibly save him from the worst when it came to sentencing?

Kowerd, as it happened, was well-prepared for Geavis' call. "Doesn't surprise me at all," he said. "I've been following the live stream. Not going well, is it?"

Within a couple of hours, Kowerd was sitting at a small table opposite Geavis, with a pair of prison officers looking on, closely.

"You're going wrong because you're confronting the jury," he said. "You're making it easy for them because you are setting yourself up as their opponent. You need to surprise them, to win their sympathy. You might not like the idea of a jury of children deciding this case; I might not like it, either. But that is the system, and you've got to work with it. Play it right and they are going to be sensitive. But you're hardening them when you've got to loosen them up."

"How do I do that?"

"Show a bit of humility. You need to impress upon them that you've been wrong – and that you know you've been wrong."

"Wrong? But I cannot have them and their table of experts rewriting climatic history at whim."

151

"Depends how long you're happy to spend in prison, I guess."

"I don't want to spend any more time in prison."

"Well, then, you've got to game this case, not treat it as an affront to your intellectual pride."

"I can't betray myself just to flatter a jury."

"Then I can't help you, I'm afraid. I would like to, but I can't. Sorry to have wasted your time. Or rather, my time."

Kowerd got up to go, but he had taken only a few steps before Geavis called him back.

"Tell me how you would approach it," Geavis said.

"Look, these kids. They are utterly convinced that the Earth is heading for a massive disaster. Lots of people are. You've got to say that you, too, have belatedly realised it. You've got to take that line even if it disgusts you."

"Is that it?"

"We've got to set up a narrative. You got it wrong for so many years because you'd been fooled by this company you worked for. They brainwashed you. They brainwashed everyone who worked for them. You were their victim. But now you are free from their evil influence you realise just how much you got it wrong."

"How could I say that, after all the things I've said already?"

"You leave it to me, that's what. I'll speak on your behalf."

"I don't have to say anything?"

"I'll tell you when to speak and you'll say what I tell you to."

The horror of it seemed at first too much for Geavis to contemplate. But what if he bit his tongue and went through with what Kowerd was suggesting? How much would it hurt him? It would be a horrible few hours, but if he were to escape with his freedom, and never had to come near this court again, never had to speak in public again, would that be a price worth paying?

His mind wandered: he was back in Brazil again, living the life to which he and Olivia had so nearly managed to escape. Maybe it could still happen. Or, if not, there was always the prospect of a quiet life back in Essex.

But there was one thing of which he became convinced. If he was going to employ Kowerd, it would only be worth it if the lawyer managed to get him out and keep him out of jail.

"I don't want to be handing over my life savings just to spend five, rather than 10, years behind bars," he told Kowerd. "Tell me you can get me off a prison sentence altogether."

"I think a suspended sentence for the offences for which you have already been convicted is a very clear possibility. So long as you are prepared to be humble."

As Geavis, still a little reluctantly, signed a document to entrust his defence to Michael Kowerd, he had flashbacks to his career at Albion Oil. He guessed he would have to agree to say whatever Kowerd told him to – even if it meant him having to lie that Albion Oil had brainwashed him. The truth was that he had been proud to work for the company, and struggled still to see it as the evil empire it was now almost universally portrayed as.

Geavis worried only that Kowerd had brainwashed him instead.

12

It was normal for Amber to lie in on a Saturday morning, and not uncommon for the extra sleep to make her more sullen. Yet still her mother, father and grandmother were unprepared for how the absence of her favourite quinoa would affect her.

"Why haven't we got any?" she said. "You know I asked for it."

"I am sorry, but there's none in the shops," said Chloe. "It has been hard to get any food at all these past few days. The shops are empty. It's just corn flakes. You'll have to make do with them."

"But they're not pure," said Amber. "I can't eat them."

"Pure or not, they're all we've got. It's them or go hungry."

Amber chose hunger rather than compromise the purity of her diet. No, she wasn't going to sully herself with food which had been banished from her approved list. Others might dilute their principles, but not her. It was hand-planted, hand-harvested quinoa or nothing. She had rarely felt so much self-worth as she slammed her bedroom door behind her and sank back onto the bed.

Her anger seemed to be sustaining her; the empty feeling in her stomach was briefly gone – though it would return with a vengeance later.

Back in the kitchen, her parents felt it best they left her alone for a bit, but Chloe lost no time in finally making a decision she had been putting off for several weeks. "I'm going to try and get her an appointment at the eating disorders clinic this week," she said. "We can't go on like this. She'll be seriously ill."

"It's a fine line," said Adam. "It's good that she's concerned about the planet, but really, it's gone too far. You've got to be able to function as a human being. Those protesters she's been associating with, they've tipped her over the edge. They don't realise what they're doing to her impressionable young mind."

"But the food shortages confirm what they've been telling her," said Olivia. "We've had a failed harvest, just as they said we would."

"Failed harvest? Don't fall for the propaganda, Mum."

"But it's true. The prime minister said so. Last year was an excessively average summer caused by the climate cataclysm, and that has affected the harvest."

"You believe that? It's a tale to fob us off, I reckon. It's the power cuts, isn't it? And the shortage of fuel for the tractors. That's what the farmers are saying, if you listen to them."

"Oh, don't you start. You'll get yourself into trouble, just like your father. He's the root of all this, as far as I'm concerned. I told him not to go on the radio and spout about the climate. It's just not worth it. It's him who's upset Amber. If he had just kept quiet, none of this would have happened."

Olivia carried on feeling negatively towards her husband for much of the morning. He had been selfish, that's what – put his own intellectual pride above the interests of his family. What had there been to gain from putting his head above the parapet and criticising the weather forecasters? Nothing. What had there been to lose? As was now evident, just about everything: a broken family, and possibly the rest of his life in jail.

She started to hate him for it, and even began faintly to contemplate divorce as she took Amber into central London, to see if they could find some quinoa there. She knew a few shops that might have it – and she reckoned it would do Amber good to get out of the flat.

Olivia and Amber emerged from the underground at Embankment station, to find themselves in the midst of a bad-tempered march several thousand people strong. "What's going on?" she asked one of the hundreds of police officers lining the street.

"It's the hunger march," she was told. "Not enough in their tummies, so they're going to Downing Street to complain about it."

Reading the banners, Olivia could see what the officer meant. "Fuel for our tractors or no food for the people!" read one. "Yes to fuel. No to hunger!" read another.

Amber couldn't believe what she was reading. "Why do they want fuel?" she asked her grandmother. "Surely they can see it's burning fuel that's ruined the climate and made everyone hungry?"

The mood among the marchers was already restive as they passed along the Embankment, but as they reached Parliament Square and met with the Huddle for Love activists, things rapidly deteriorated. The police, trying to keep the two groups apart, ended up being squeezed. They were pushed, shoved, bombarded by missiles.

"Stop the climate criminals!" shouted the activists.

"Give us our fuel allowances now!" the marchers roared back.

The hunger marchers found a man selling pancakes from a cart and accused him of being a black marketeer. "Bloody spiv!" they shouted, as he fled over Westminster Bridge, before scooping up his pancakes and gobbling them down as if they had not eaten for a week. It was an incident that would be picked over a few days later, as the 50 or so people arrested that day on public order offences were put through the courts.

But for the leader of the march, Dave Bodger, the consequences were more serious. Climbing on the railings outside the Houses of Parliament, he started to make a speech.

"We haven't come to be lectured on the climate by a bunch of hippies," he shouted through his megaphone. "We've come to lay out the facts. This country is starving because we can't get fuel for the tractors."

There was a roar from the crowd. "Stop lying to us and give us the fuel permits."

A senior police officer, who was filming the disturbance, pricked up his ears at that sentence. "Stop lying to us" – what did he mean by that? Did he mean stop lying to us about the climate apocalypse? And if so, was that not tantamount to climate change denial?

A few minutes later, officers moved forwards and arrested Bodger. They hoped that by removing him from the scene they might succeed in breaking up the march. But instead, it enraged the marchers even more. Running battles took place for a couple of hours, in which several buildings were set alight – with each side blaming the other.

Fortunately, the riot was missed by Olivia, who had sensed trouble and swiftly took Amber away in the opposite direction, to Covent Garden. They didn't find the quinoa they were looking for, but with gentle persuasion Amber accepted some porridge oats instead – even if the vendor selling them from a cart, at three times the normal price, couldn't vouch for their having been grown and harvested without the help of fossil fuel-powered machinery.

See, Olivia told herself, that's all Amber needs: a bit of time and space. How awful to be thinking of sending her to a clinic for eating disorders.

However, Olivia questioned her own judgement the following day when Amber refused to rise from her bed at all, saying: "what's the point, when we're all going to be dead soon?"

*

In his cell at Highdown Prison, Geavis quietly welcomed Bodger's arrest. "It'll take the heat off my own trial, now they've got themselves a bigger fish," he told himself. "Why go after me?"

But he was fooling himself. As the climate court reconvened on Monday morning, there were just as many activists waiting outside as there had been the previous week. The audience following the live streaming of the trial had grown still further. Everyone knew that today would bring the biggest verdict on Geavis so far: that of the manslaughter of the 35 people killed in the Guy Fawkes night storm.

Before the jury of the future returned to its deliberations, Michael Kowerd was on his feet, announcing that he was now representing the accused.

"I have a statement to make," he told them. "My client recognises the seriousness of the offence with which he is charged. He fully accepts the reality of the climate apocalypse and asks you to disregard any statements that he might have made in the past which left any ambiguity in the matter. He is truly sorry for the contribution that he has personally made towards the climate apocalypse. It is to his eternal shame and regret that he entered into the career that he did.

"But he wishes to make known one thing. That during his time working for Albion Oil he was under intense pressure to disbelieve that the activities of the company were in any way harmful to the Earth's climate. Bullying tactics within the company created a climate of their own: a climate of fear. In this closed, threatening atmosphere it was little wonder that he came to believe the lies he was told. He is, in his own way, a victim of a toxic corporate culture."

Geavis sat and listened, aghast. No, no, this isn't right, he told himself. I can't put my name to this. He shook his head over and over again – a gesture he worried was giving away the insincerity of Kowerd's statement, but which he later realised was being taken by some on the jury as proof of what Kowerd was saying – that here was a man deep in regret for his past career.

Geavis was desperate to intervene. He wanted to ask Kowerd why he wasn't emphasising how he had attempted to save lives during the storm by raising the alarm among the seaside bungalows. Geavis could hardly bear to listen as Kowerd spoke on.

"Mr Geavis, who is an inadequate figure in many respects, sadly did not have the ability to resist the propaganda that was fed to him. Indeed, as you have heard, he promulgated some of it himself in his capacity as a press officer – a job he did not want and at which he did not excel. But all this said, it remains true, does it not, that – as the experts have told you – the Guy Fawkes Night storm cannot be wholly attributed to the man-made climate apocalypse. Other storms in the future, for sure, might be attributed to the emissions spewed out by Albion Oil. But this particular storm was of a magnitude that could have happened by chance. Therefore, it would be quite wrong for you to condemn him for the death and destruction which resulted from it. I understand your anger – your justified anger – at those who have stolen your futures from you by aiding and abetting the climate apocalypse. It is quite right that they should face the music, be brought to account, be made to pay for their despicable actions. And pay they will! But Mr Geavis – a vulnerable and pathetic figure, as I have said – is a very poor substitute for the far more senior oil executives, whom you understandably want to punish. So I say, look at this pitiful man, worn down by years of abuse from the evil firm that employed him, and dare to be gentle with him. Take it out not on him, but on the bigger people, who will no doubt be brought before this court in the near future."

As Geavis trembled with angst and anger, members of the jury began their deliberations, their mood palpably changed by Kowerd's address.

"So, said Misha," we couldn't make our mind up on Friday. What do we think now?"

"I can quite imagine the pressure he was under," said Morgan. "Any of us could have fallen for it. The poor man was tortured and cajoled into believing the lies fed to him."

"He still should have known," said Bunty.

"But if they were threatening him?"

"Why didn't he leave?"

"Maybe he couldn't," said Sam. "Maybe they wouldn't let him."

"Or maybe he was just greedy and wanted the money," said Bunty.

"But did he cause the storm anyway?" said Misha. "If it could have happened by chance then we can't be sure, as we talked about on Friday."

"Can you imagine what it was like working at that company?" came a voice down the table. "We've got to put ourselves in his shoes."

"I'd love to think I'd have been brave enough to tell them what they were doing was wrong," said Morgan. "But I can't be sure. I might have folded like he did."

"I'd definitely have told them to stuff their oil," said Bunty. "And I wouldn't have gone to work for the company in the first place. Why did he do that?"

There was a thoughtful pause before Sam spoke up. "My followers think he's guilty."

"What?" said Misha.

"I asked my followers on Mob what they thought, and they're 98 percent in favour that we convict him."

"But we were told not to do that, don't you remember?"

Kowerd was quickly on his feet. "This must not stand!" he said. "For a member of the jury to consult people outside the courtroom is strictly

159

forbidden. The case and the jury must be dismissed. My client must be acquitted."

The table of legal experts agreed that such an indiscretion by a member of the jury would cause the case to collapse in any other court, but the climate court had been constituted with a different set of rules. The legislation establishing it did not make it clear whether a jury of the future was forbidden to consult social media or not. Kowerd was adamant that the case could not be allowed to go on. But after more than an hour of its own deliberations the table of legal experts had some advice for Misha, which she read out.

"It is not permissible for members of the jury of the future to consult anyone outside this courtroom when it comes to making its decision. It is not, however, the case that the jury must be dismissed. Members must disregard what they have been heard on social media and make their decision based purely on evidence presented in this courtroom."

That seemed to settle it. The jury felt able to decide – and felt compelled to ignore the advice from Sam's followers on Mob.

A few minutes later, Misha came forward. "We find Mr Geavis not guilty of the manslaughter of the 35 people killed in the Guy Fawkes Night storm".

Geavis supposed that he ought to feel relieved, yet he felt nothing at all. Had today's proceedings really been part of the same trial he had sat through for a week? He had tried to reason with the jury, tried to have a constructive debate with them on anything from the causes of storms to the progress of climate change and it had got him nowhere. Then, Kowerd had come in and turned the case around with a blatant appeal to the children's emotions. It had got him off a serious charge, but at what price?

"You've been acquitted of manslaughter," Kowerd said to him after the court had wound up for the day. "You could *try* to look pleased."

"Of course I'm pleased," said Geavis. "I'm just a bit stunned, that's all."

But in truth, he knew he wasn't pleased. On previous days, when he had been convicted of charges, he had gone back to the prison still with some fight in him. If he was going to be jailed, he had thought, then at least it would be with the satisfaction of knowing he had stood up for something: for scientific reason and, indeed, for his own integrity. He didn't have that anymore; it had been sucked out of him by Kowerd's act of theatre. He had won, but won dirty. Was being pitied better than being hated? He wasn't sure. All he knew was that both were a long, long way from being respected.

Misha left court in a pensive mood. The decision had been a serious challenge, she thought to herself, but she was sure she had done the right thing. How revealing it had been to see Geavis' vulnerable side. Up until now she had never understood how adults could involve themselves in the evil fossil fuel business, but now, she thought, she was beginning to appreciate how some had come to do so without necessarily being bad people. It had been different for them, perhaps. They had grown up at a time when so many people were doing foolish things to the planet and not thinking for a moment about it. Nothing could excuse what they had done, but perhaps it was true what the lawyer had said: people like Geavis were victims, too.

Halfway back to her hotel, however, she began to question herself. Thanks to weekend riot, Misha's police escort had been doubled to eight armoured vehicles. From the patched-up window of her sedan chair she couldn't see the crowds as clearly as she had on previous days, but what she could see disturbed her. There was no-one cheering her this time, and many were shaking their heads.

Back in her hotel room she couldn't finish the film her parents had selected in the hope of relaxing her. It seemed so childish and silly – she wasn't interested in cartoon animal stories anymore. But above that, she was still upset by the reaction of the crowds. She knew she was not supposed to check her feed on Mob until the trial had been concluded, but she could not stop herself looking.

When she did, she was aghast at what some people were saying.

"Maybe we shouldn't have trusted it to children after all," was a typical comment, from someone who hid their real identity behind the name Wat Tyler. "Can't believe he's been let off. We had him in our sights!" Another wrote: "No justice for Deptford. How sick can you get?" Others looked forward to the one remaining charge against Geavis, that of ecocide. "Won't be accepting court verdict if he doesn't go down for killing the birds," wrote one. "It'll be time for action!"

But what action? Another who had posted their thoughts seemed to provide an answer. "Can we sue the jury of the future for denial if it acquits the bogus meteorologist of ecocide?"

Misha gulped when she read that remark, asking herself: what have we done? We let him off and yet so many people think he was guilty. Had she missed something which was obvious to the thousands of people who had watched the live stream?

She went through the day's events over and over again in her head. Yes, of course, she thought: we hardly considered the victims of the storm at all – the lawyer had made us concentrate on Geavis, making us feel sorry for him, to the point we forgot about the 35 dead. What an awful omission it seemed. The only consolation she could think of was that there was still one more charge, so there was still an opportunity to put things right.

Misha hardly slept that night and felt weak as she took her seat in the hotel's gilded dining room for breakfast the following morning. She knew she shouldn't be looking at her Mob feed, but again, she couldn't stop herself. She needed to know what was being said about her.

There were plenty more negative remarks, but, to her surprise, she found herself able to read through them with becoming upset. But just as her vegan sausages were being served by a waiter in white gloves, she came across something she found it impossible to ignore.

"Oh my God!" she exclaimed, leading the waiter to stumble and drop her sausages.

She read the words: "I'm going to starve myself if Bryan Geavis isn't convicted of ecocide." Then, beneath the comment, she read the name of its author. It was her friend, Amber.

"Everything alright, miss?" asked the waiter.

Misha hardly heard him as she left the table and ran up to the privacy of her room. "No, Amber, don't do it!" she hurriedly messaged her friend. But would Amber get to read it?

Amber's post had already gone viral and she had been inundated with responses, most of them supportive. "Go for it, Amber," said one. "We're behind you. Let's get pressure on the jury to send evil Geavis down for life and you can go back to eating your favourite foods again." Another said:

"You're the best, Amber. Fingers crossed for you. I'll buy you ice cream if he's convicted."

Misha tore at her hair in frustration. "No, no!" she cried out. "Don't Amber, don't!"

But what could she do? She had to prepare for the day's court proceedings. She sent several more messages to Amber, and, with tears in her eyes, was still messaging from her sedan chair as it drew up outside the climate court. She was looking out for a reply until the moment she walked into the courtroom, but none came.

Tired and in turmoil, Misha kept having to stop as she read out the words on the piece of paper before her, confirming what everyone knew already: that Geavis had been charged with ecocide through the killing of a colony of birds on the Thames marshes during the Guy Fawkes Night storm.

She had hardly finished when Kowerd was up on his feet, demanding to make his point.

"Surely," he said, "the court has already established that the storm of the fifth of November last year was an event with natural causes, that it cannot be blamed on man-made emissions? If so, then it is illogical to go ahead with the ecocide charge, because it depends on the same, disproven premise. How can it be argued that Albion Oil had been responsible for the deaths of seabirds when it has been judged not to have caused the deaths of 35 people a few miles away in the same incident?"

This argument threw Misha, who, dazed and confused, looked to her legal advisers for guidance. After much debate at the table, Misha relayed their advice.

"The charge of ecocide must be heard on its own merits," read Misha from the notes prepared for her. "Whatever conclusion members of the jury came to on the previous charge, we must consider the issues afresh."

Kowerd was not pleased but had little choice other than to accept the situation. Geavis sat dispassionately. Misha then called Bryony Smart, a celebrated maker of TV documentaries on the natural world, to explain what had happened.

A couple of weeks before the storm, Smart explained, a colony of 500 or so dark-bellied Brent geese had arrived from Siberia at their usual place

163

for overwintering: the nature reserve known as the Broad Washes, which had previously been mentioned in the case.

"They were extremely tired after their 2000-mile migration," Smart explained, "but that should not have been a problem, as food is normally plentiful on the marshes at that time of year. But unfortunately, while they were still trying to establish themselves, the flood waters inundated their feeding grounds. A hundred or so birds were caught in the surging waters and drowned instantly, and another 200 succumbed to hunger over the next few days as their feeding grounds had been destroyed.

"We can only imagine how traumatic it must have been for them. They're exhausted after flying so far; they just need to eat and eat. And then suddenly, the marshes on which they depend are taken away from beneath their feet. Many would have been youngsters on their first journey to the Essex marshes, and then this happens. Can you think what it must have been like for their mums and dads?"

Several members of the jury were in tears, including Misha, who was almost choking as she asked: "And was this the fault of Albion Oil?"

"In my opinion, yes," said Smart. "Our storms seem to be getting stronger and stronger. And if you're a blameless little bird, that's a problem. As far as I'm concerned, these poor little creatures were killed as a direct result of carbon emissions from fossil fuel burning. It's heartbreaking, isn't it?"

Geavis glanced across to Kowerd. Surely he wasn't going to let that stand. Just four days ago the table of experts had given the jury the advice that the storm was a random event which could not be attributed to climate change, and yet here was one of their number – and surely not an expert in climate, either – who was trying to overrule the earlier opinion. But Kowerd chose not to make an issue of this, and allowed Smart to continue:

"I wonder if you can imagine being one of those geese. You're used to the tide coming in and out, but you know where you can retreat to. And then suddenly, these great waves get whipped up. We know these wonderfully intelligent birds communicate with each other. I wonder what they were saying to each other as they started to get into difficulty and saw their brothers and sisters becoming overwhelmed by the floodwaters and drowning. It doesn't bear thinking about, does it? These are birds, living in harmony with nature, and we've suddenly destroyed their habitat and killed their friends. They must hate us for it."

Full of tears, Misha asked Geavis whether he realised the extent of the death and destruction the floodwaters had caused. Geavis could hardly contain himself, but it was Kowerd who insisted on rising to speak in his place.

"We have just heard a heart-rending account of what happened to the avian population of the Thames Estuary. It is not in question that wading birds are facing the brunt of rising sea levels which are destroying their marshlands – even if, as I ask you to remember, it has already been established by this court that the Guy Fawkes Night storm cannot itself be blamed on the activities of Albion Oil or any other man-made cause. Birds are vulnerable creatures and deserve our utmost care; too often they do not receive it. You are right to be angry and upset at how they are so callously treated.

"But I ask you to consider: who was it that restored this stretch of marshland for the birds in the first place? Who was it that turned a poisoned stretch of riverside into a nature reserve where the birds could feed and spend the winter? The man who did this is sitting in this room. He is the accused."

Geavis was stunned. No, no, that wasn't right. It hadn't been his idea to create a nature reserve; he had merely been the PR man who had blown Albion Oil's trumpet for it. He hadn't even wanted the job. It had been a stopgap, to get him through to retirement. Could Kowerd really get away with telling such a fib?

Yet, however uneasy Geavis felt, Kowerd went on.

"Mr Geavis is a man who found himself embroiled in an evil industry, up to his neck in activities which he came to realise were killing the Earth. He didn't leave his job – as you might think he ought to have done. But he did something, nonetheless, which ought to be applauded: he used what influence he could to undo just a little of the damage which the company had wrought on nature. He took the site of its oil refinery and created a sanctuary for the birds, a little Eden in the midst of a Stygian landscape of doom. Of course, as we now know, the nature reserve known as the Broad Washes turned out not to be quite the sanctuary that was hoped. But that couldn't have been foreseen.

It was just plain bad luck that this flood – a random event, I remind you – happened to occur when the birds were at their weakest and most vulnerable. It was a tragedy, let us be clear, but one for which Mr Geavis cannot be blamed."

Misha, who had been listening intently, was beginning to look less and less impressed. "But you told us yesterday that Mr Geavis was pathetic. How come now you're telling us he's a hero?"

"Mr Geavis is a man of many parts," said Kowerd. "He can be one thing one day and another thing another day. But it is irrefutable that he was on the side of nature and not on the side of the destroyers, even if he may technically have been under their employment."

Misha then turned back to Smart for some guidance. "Is it right that the Broad Washes were an important nature reserve?"

"Oh, Misha," she said. "I was here on another day when Mr Geavis himself described the project to restore these marshes as nothing more than greenwashing – a brazen attempt to launder Albion Oil's filthy reputation. This was no nature reserve; it was a death trap. And as a result, several hundred loving, sociable creatures with families just like yours and mine were cruelly cut down in their prime. Albion Oil failed these creatures in the most hideous way imaginable."

Now Morgan had a question. "Mr Geavis, was it really your idea to create the nature reserve? I thought you said the other day that it was just your job to publicise it."

Kowerd was up on his feet in a flash and launching himself into his spiel so quickly that he felt a little dizzy, but still it was not quick enough to smother the words "that's right," uttered by Geavis.

"Mr Geavis was an instrumental part of this project which, contrary to what the witness claims, provided a home for several generations of birds before the tragic events of the fifth of November – the tragic *random* events, unrelated to the climate apocalypse, as you have already established."

The jury of the future now entered its deliberations on the final charge. It did so while several members were still sobbing.

"Those poor birds," came one voice. "It does my head in just listening to it."

A girl shook her head. "It's so shameful. I can't believe what we do to the birds. Why can't we share the planet with them, rather than treating it as our own property?"

"I really don't buy it that this storm wasn't caused by Albion Oil," said Bunty. "Storms don't just happen. We used not to have them. The experts told us that last week. People used to imagine storms, but they only actually started happening when we began burning fossil fuels."

"Is that right?" asked Morgan. "Maybe we always used to have storms but they're much worse now than they used to be."

"It's just so wrong to kill birds," said Sam. "They haven't done anything wrong. If there's anyone who deserves to be drowned, it's us."

"Not *us*," said Bunty. "The people from the oil companies. It's not *our* fault."

"We can't let this go. We've got to make a stand," said Misha. "There are people out there counting on us to get it right. We must send a really powerful message to the polluters that no, you're not getting away with it. Justice is going to catch up with you."

"That's right," said Bunty. "We won't be forgiven if we get this wrong. We'll be as bad as the oil company people."

"I guess you're right," said Morgan. "We don't want to give the impression we're on their side."

It didn't take much longer for the jury to take a vote and for Misha to deliver its verdict.

Bryan Geavis was guilty of ecocide, just about the most serious offence of which anyone could be convicted.

13

The last exchange between Geavis and Kowerd before the former was taken back to prison was a brief and sombre affair.

"I don't know what to say," said Kowerd. "I really thought we had a chance on the ecocide charge."

"What now?"

"The good news is I might still be able to save you from a long jail sentence. I'll be arguing very robustly before sentencing. That's not for a few days, so we've got time to work something out."

"You think so?"

"It's all a bit hit and miss with the climate court. Our whole legal system – our whole system of democracy – is supposed to be based on logic and reason. How do we cope when it is all reduced to a welter of emotion? The only way I can see through this is to play people at their own game."

Geavis thought Kowerd might be right in this, but he wasn't paying him to come up with interesting observations; he wanted to keep out of prison, and on this Kowerd had failed him. But what could he say?

Geavis put up no resistance as security staff ushered him away and bundled him into a van, which was repeatedly thumped by a jeering crowd.

A couple of hours later he was back in prison, though an unfamiliar part. "Why not the usual cell?" he asked.

"We've got to be careful now," said an officer, taking him up a corridor into an isolated wing. "There's a lot of inmates who don't take kindly to convicted animal killers."

While Geavis had not made many friends in prison, he still felt deeply the absence of other people that evening, when he was made to sit and eat his supper alone. He had decided long ago that he did not want too much to do with criminals if he could help it, but even so he now realised that he needed brief interactions with other people to stimulate his mind. He needed to see them, to hear them, to share some sort of camaraderie even if he found it hard to converse with them – otherwise, he was going to go mad.

For weeks, he had managed to convince himself that he wasn't a real criminal. But now, he had to face up to the reality that in many prisoners' eyes – in the eyes of the law, indeed – he was among the worst offenders of the lot.

*

As for Misha, she felt she ought to be enjoying the ride back to her hotel more than she was. Most people in the crowd were cheering her again. Yet she knew she had had enough of the attention. She remembered fondly the days when she could go about the streets unrecognised, unbothered, being a normal 12-year-old girl. The crowd might be on her side now, but she had seen the previous day how quickly its mood could change, and it disturbed her.

It didn't feel right to soak up the adulation, so instead she sank back into the deep velvet upholstery of her sedan chair and scrolled through the feed on her Mob account. But that, too, nauseated her. Where once she would have been flattered to receive a message from Zoe Fluff, now it irritated her.

"Just gotta get back to London to celebrate with our heroine from the jury of the future," Fluff had written. "Great work, Misha! Took a flight over the Himalayas today and saw for myself the melting glaciers. Just been told that the yeti is in danger of going extinct. So heartbreaking! Got to get more of the men responsible for this to face up to their crimes."

Misha was less confident of her own achievements. She wondered whether she had really done anything to help the climate. A man was going to go to jail for a very long time, but she found herself involuntarily asking what good it would do. Perhaps it would deter others from ruining the climate: there was that to be said for it. But then, there was no oil industry left anyway.

The newspapers were no less forgiving than were the users of Mob. "Oilman Did Cause Fatal Storm," read the front page of the *Daily Torrent*. "Now He'll Pay for Massacre of Innocent Seabirds."

The news of Geavis' conviction for ecocide smothered the other big news story of the day: another protest by a crowd of angry farmers. This time it was a smaller group, but the 100 or so marchers did manage to achieve what others had failed to do on the previous Saturday: a few of them managed to gain an audience with the prime minister.

"I think we ought to invite them in," said Downwood. "We invited in the Huddle for Love camp, so we should give the farmers a hearing, too." A group of three representatives was selected and let through the gates for the short walk to Number 10.

"It's getting desperate," a spokesman told the prime minister. "Without fuel, we can't plant crops, and without that there'll be no harvest. We can't take much more of this. We've got farms going bankrupt like nobody's business."

Downwood said she was sympathetic and would see what she could do – bearing in mind, of course, the government's commitment to its carbon reduction targets. "Without taking very serious action on that, the land may become barren and we will end up with no farming industry at all, if the climate continues to heat up," she replied.

The farmers' spokesman was unsatisfied by this. "It's a matter of absolute urgency," he said. Downwood acknowledged that he was right: there was not a moment to lose in the fight against climate change. But on further pleading she agreed that perhaps she would be able to find money in the kitty for extra grants towards electric tractors. But what about those who farmed on heavy soil, for whom the electric tractors currently on the market had proved unsatisfactory? Eventually, Downwood agreed that the Department for the Climate Apocalypse would try to find a way of cutting emissions more sharply elsewhere in order to grant the farmers a little extra in the way of diesel permits in the short term.

When the idea was discussed with the citizens' cabinet, however, Evie Wilks was having none of it.

"Why are you even meeting with the polluters?" she asked. "If you think there's two sides of a debate in this, you don't understand. There's no debate. Either we change our ways, or we die. And you'd better start taking that on board."

Wilks, it turned out, had come with a plan. That farms were going bankrupt presented the government with an opportunity, she argued. Why not pick up the land and the buildings at a substantial discount and set up community farms which would practice zero-carbon farming? Machinery could be eliminated: the farms would be worked entirely by human hand. Cherish the land rather than rape it, and it would produce more food.

"An interesting idea," said Downwood. "Perhaps it would make a worthwhile experiment. It would certainly be a way of getting these farms back into production very quickly."

And so, in spite of reservations from her advisers, who pointed out that it was far from clear where sufficient workers could be recruited, and that hand cultivation would seriously increase the cost of producing food, an order was quickly drawn up empowering the Department for the Climate Apocalypse to seize bankrupt farms and organise them into the beginnings of a new national food service.

Public sympathy for the farmers was, in any case, beginning to fade as the food crisis started to resolve itself. Overseas producers, sensing the money to be made in hungry Britain, began to divert their exports there. The first stocks to arrive in the shops were eagerly taken up by hoarders, who were prepared to pay fancy prices. Some of the imports were fully registered so that the carbon emissions spewed out in producing them were properly recorded, but others were not. Given the need to avert shortages, officials were minded to turn a blind eye in all but the worst excesses of the black market. Yet after a week or two, the situation began to change. So many ships laden with produce began to arrive at the country's ports that soon there was an opposite problem: a glut. The black marketeers were so aggrieved at the loss of business that, seeking someone to blame, a band of them visited Dave Bodger late one night and threatened him. "Don't you dare get your rabble out on the streets again," he was told. "They're our food shortages. They're nothing to do with you, right?"

*

Over in Beckton, Amber had agreed to celebrate her grandfather's conviction by eating a few dry biscuits. Yet it wasn't to last. Her eating disorder continued to be an all-consuming challenge for her family. At every meal either her father, mother or grandmother would sit with her, trying to persuade her to eat. Generally she would, eventually, but not until she had been convinced that the production of the food she was agreeing to eat had not harmed the environment in any way.

First, she needed to know how many carbon emissions were associated with the product. This was easy enough because the necessary information was printed on the side of every food packet, to help people fill in their carbon returns. But Amber needed to know that no animals had been harmed in its production and that no other environmental damage had been caused. This required much searching on the internet, and even then Amber was not always happy, continually questioning whether such information was accurate.

"Don't take my phone away, Grandma," she said after one especially trying breakfast. "It says that over-production of quinoa is harming the llamas. They don't have enough land to graze."

For weeks, quinoa had been the only breakfast she would eat, but now it had to be discarded completely from her diet. After two days of eating no breakfast at all she agreed to eat some sorghum porridge – to the relief of her parents, who had travelled several miles to buy it.

Olivia, tired of the daily chore of persuading Amber to eat, grew less and less tolerant of her granddaughter, on occasions raising her voice and bringing the girl to tears. But every time she did so she was instantly filled with guilt. No, it wasn't fair to blame the child. She was merely the victim of the circumstances in which she was being brought up. Everyone seemed to be perpetually anxious about the effect that their existence was having on the planet, so it was hardly a surprise if an impressionable young girl had taken it to extremes.

But there was one person who *was* responsible for tipping her over the edge. Bryan. Were it not for his behaviour – in court and before that, at Adam's flat – then it would never have come to this.

The news of his conviction for ecocide had tipped Olivia over her own, personal edge. Their marriage hadn't been right for years, she told herself. But on they had ploughed, neither quite motivated enough to bring it to an end. Now he had been convicted, it was the jolt she needed.

That same evening she wrote him a letter, informing him that it was all over and she was seeking a divorce. She then went out to post it, keen to do so before she had a chance to change her mind.

Later on, awake in the middle of the night, she was disturbed by doubts. What had she done? Here he was, in greater need than he had ever been in their married life, and she was abandoning him! Was there a way to get that letter back before it reached him? Could she get her arm inside the post box and get it out?

She thought about it again and again, for several hours while she turned over and over in bed. She kept asking herself: was his conviction fair? No, of course it wasn't. The government had wanted to make an example of a climate change denier and he had just happened to fit the bill. But then again, he had brought it upon himself by being foolish. He must have known what would happen once he started to berate the weather forecasters; he had been asking for trouble. Even so, was it right that he should be punished for being foolish?

Finally, around dawn, she fell asleep. When she woke up, to conduct another breakfast vigil with Amber, all seemed clearer. Yes, she was right to have written that letter, she told herself. However miserable and unfair Bryan's fate, it wasn't wrong to think of herself. And she knew the right thing for her was to extract herself from the marriage and start afresh. Still, she left it a day or two before visiting a solicitor – but she never suffered such doubts again as she had that night.

*

Geavis had not received his wife's letter by the time he was driven off to be sentenced. Nor was Olivia much on his mind. He could no longer connect with his situation. When he had merely been facing a fine, even when he knew he was likely to be jailed for up to 10 years, he could contemplate his fate. He could think what it would mean to be incarcerated for a decade.

He looked back a decade and thought of everything that had happened in that time. He could dare to imagine one day being released.

But a life sentence? The finality of it sent him into deep despair which evolved into apathy. What did anything matter anymore? His life was over, and that was that.

He was still in this frame of mind when he took to the dock in the climate court for one last time. He was pleased to have a lawyer speaking on his behalf, because he didn't feel up to it himself.

Kowerd was back in confident form. "You have it in your power to jail this man for a very long time," he told the jury, waving a hand in Geavis' direction. "Indeed, you may feel that you are expected to hand down a long jail sentence. You may receive plaudits if you do so. But before you come to decide on an appropriate sentence, I ask you to think of this. Mr Geavis is a contrite man. He has been bruised by the proceedings of this court. He is a shell of his former self. He cuts a sad figure and yet he deserves little sympathy, because it is beyond question that he committed a very grave offence in causing the death of a colony of seabirds. You have quite rightly convicted him on that charge, showing your true maturity in the way you have questioned him over the past few days. You have each helped the world become a better place, and you are all to be congratulated for that.

"But in your last duty in this court you have the opportunity to do something even greater, by asking yourselves: what would be gained by jailing Mr Geavis? Where, you must ask yourselves, would he be of most use to society: rotting away in jail for next decade or however long he has left to live, or by employing him in an educational capacity? Mr Geavis, should you allow him the chance, has the potential to become a great asset in the fight against the climate apocalypse. He is a living warning to us all not to forget nature, not to get so carried away with our own self-enrichment and self-importance that we end up treating the planet with reckless abandon. Think of the powerful message it would send to others if you put him before an audience and allowed him to explain how he fell into depravity. Who, listening to a contrite Bryan Geavis, would not start to reassess their own lives and ask themselves: what more could I do for the planet?

"Now, you may choose to jail Mr Geavis – and no-one could blame you if you took that decision. But I simply ask you to consider the more imaginative option of keeping him out of jail and imposing on him instead a requirement for community service. Let him keep his freedom, but on the condition that he regularly makes himself available to humble himself before the public. He asks no payment for this; it will be a big enough reward for him to know that he has helped atone for his sins a little by pleading to others not to follow the course that he himself followed."

Kowerd then sat down, leaving the jury of the future to begin what were to become long hours of deliberation.

All members seemed confused at first. They had thought a formality that they send him to jail, yet the more they thought about it, the more they came to see things the way the lawyer had asked them to. They consulted with their own table of lawyers, then talked among themselves, then consulted again. A conversation then opened between them.

"Is he really that sorry?" asked Bunty. "He hasn't shown us much regret. He hasn't said a damn word since he brought in that lawyer."

"Maybe that's why he hasn't said anything," suggested Sam. "He's so upset about what he did."

"Or he needs someone else to express his own remorse for him because he's not really upset at all," said Bunty.

Misha, who had been unusually quiet, allowed her mind to wander. What would people say on Mob if they refused to jail Geavis? Would she receive abuse again? But no, she thought, that wasn't the right way to think about it. To hell with rude people on Mob. It wasn't their decision to decide what happens to Geavis; it was a decision of the jury of the future alone. As the lawyer had said, they had to take a mature attitude towards it all.

"I think we should take this idea of a community sentence really seriously," she said. "The accused could help people see how serious the climate apocalypse is and how wrong it is to deny it."

"But would people listen?" asked Morgan. "I think we need to hear him – and not his lawyer – say how very sorry he is."

The others thought it an excellent idea. "Mr Geavis, can you show us how sorry you really are for denying the climate apocalypse and causing the deaths of several hundred birds?" asked Misha.

Kowerd was caught out by this demand and asked for a little time to consider how his client should respond. Geavis struggled to think what he should say, but after Kowerd had taken the trouble to coach him he managed to say a few rehearsed lines.

"I am truly sorry for my actions and recognise the full gravity of what I have done," he said slowly, as he recalled from memory what Kowerd had told him to say. "If I can help others to recognise the full gravity of the climate apocalypse and change their ways, then I think I will have done something useful."

The jury listened to his broken words, with the odd tear running down the cheeks of a couple of members.

"What do we think?" asked Misha.

"I don't like the idea of locking anyone up," said Sam. "It must get so boring."

Misha then consulted with the lawyers again, and then with the table of experts; Geavis could see they were undertaking some calculations. Finally, towards the end of the afternoon, Misha was ready to make an announcement – which had been drafted for her by the lawyers – to the court.

"Mr Geavis, we have heard representations on your behalf and have arrived at the following decision. You are sentenced to jail for life, but so long as you fulfil the conditions that we set you, the sentence will be suspended. You will not go to jail, but instead you must, upon request, and not more than once a fortnight, attend public lectures where you will express your remorse at committing the offences of which you have been convicted: denying climate change, stealing children's futures, and ecocide.

"We further find you liable to pay reparations for your role in causing the climate apocalypse. These have been assessed as follows. Your share of financial damage caused by carbon emissions comes to £2.2 billion, payable to this court, to be divided among the victims of the climate apocalypse. This must be paid with any assets you own. If you are unable to pay, then you will be declared bankrupt. You must respond to this demand within 28 days. Do you understand the sentence?"

Geavis nodded, although he was dazed by the news and it took a while to sink in. Was he really going to be spared jail? He was so pleasantly surprised by this realisation that he initially overlooked the financial implications of the court's decision. Addressing the occasional audience wouldn't be too difficult, surely? It was certainly better than jail.

It was only when Kowerd congratulated him that he remembered a financial penalty had also been imposed.

"We've done it!" said Kowerd. "I said I'd find a way – and I did. You've got your freedom. You must be pleased." He shuffled his feet a bit. "That's a pretty stiff bill for damages, though. I'm going to have to ask you to pay my bill before the court get its hands on your money. I'll be asking for a charge against your house."

The reality then dawned. Geavis asked Kowerd to repeat the figure. How on earth had anyone worked out that he owed £2.2 billion? And who were these victims, anyway? He made a request to the court and was told that that the damage caused by climate change all around the world, in the past and in the future – the suffering of victims of floods, wildfires, people who had developed chilblains from extra cold weather, anything that could even vaguely be attributed to the climate apocalypse – had been estimated, totalled up and then divided between the number of senior executives who had worked in the oil industry.

It was a fantasy figure, but it was purely academic: Geavis didn't have £2.2 billion, or anything like it. In fact, the victims of the climate apocalypse were to receive next to nothing. Once Geavis' house was sold to pay Kowerd's bill, it turned out, there would be little left.

Geavis had nothing to say to the reporters who persisted in stuffing their microphones close to his face as he left the court. "How are you going to pay the bill?" asked one. "Have you got a secret stash of money like all the other oil executives?"

The question hardly deserved an answer, and it didn't get one. Geavis resolved from now that he was going to keep his mouth shut, save for his obligatory contributions to public lectures, as outlined in his sentence.

That evening, Geavis received Olivia's letter. First his home was gone, and now his marriage, too. It was not hard to see why Olivia had made her decision, but still he berated himself for failing to see it coming.

I never even tried to keep her, did I? he thought despairingly, as he collected his few possessions from a prison locker and was shown to the gate, a free man. What a bitter kind of freedom it was. Here he was, out on street without handcuffs for the first time in months, and yet unable to savour the moment. Every little memory came like a little stab in the heart.

He would have brooded over it a bit more, had it not been for the practical problems he had to resolve. Where was he going to go? Where was he going to sleep? He couldn't go back to Essex, as his house was let out, and he could hardly beg the hospitality of his son, given that Olivia was staying at his flat. He ended up spending that first night on a bench, curled up against the cold, before moving to a bus station when it started to rain around four in the morning. The next day he managed to motivate himself to contact an old friend, who allowed him to sleep on his sofa.

The following Monday, Geavis was introduced to his probation officer, who in turn referred him to a social worker, Lindsay. She greeted him with a big smile; the first he could remember seeing in months.

"They're usually a lot younger, the people I deal with," she told him. "They're quite robust and they bounce back quick – if they don't bounce straight back to jail, that is. But we can't have you sleeping on park benches at your age."

First, she found him a bed in a bail hostel, and then went through the practical issues he faced. Although he would lose his home and all other assets, he would be allowed to keep some of his weekly pension for spending money. But how could he spend it, when he had broken the social pledge and been blocked by every shop, café and other business that used it?

Lindsay had an answer: she found out he could build up points through good behaviour and then sign the social pledge afresh. Where would he live in the longer term, and how would he occupy himself? Lindsay had a suggestion for that, too. She had just heard of an opportunity for people like him, who had just been released from jail or fallen into debt. There was a new community farm opening in Lincolnshire which would house him, feed him and pay him pocket money in return for work.

He had little hesitation in agreeing to the suggestion. The further away from London, the further away from public attention, he reasoned, the better. He rubbed between his fingers the train ticket to Lincoln that Lindsay had given him, treating it like the ticket he had once hoped would take him on the first leg of a journey to a new life in Brazil. But he knew very well that it offered a very different future.

14

Although his face was now familiar to the public, and he was used to the attention of crowds outside the climate court, Geavis correctly guessed that the fuss at King's Cross was not directed at him. In fact, with his hat pulled down so tightly that it obscured his eyebrows, he was scarcely recognised by anyone, save for a few people whose expressions indicated they thought they had seen him somewhere else, but couldn't quite work out where. It was only when he saw an entourage following him up the platform that he realised that the prime minister would be taking the same train.

Sarah Downwood was privately pleased with Geavis' conviction. It would get the Huddle for Love movement off her back for a little while, she reckoned. They had been baying for a former oil executive to be prosecuted for a while and now they had their man. The government's relations with the citizens' cabinet were now pretty good, she reflected as she settled into her first class seat and turned her mind to the speech she was going to make at the closing ceremony for Britain's last remaining cement works on the banks of the Humber.

"Ladies and gentlemen, it is with great pleasure that I come here today to formally bring an end to the nation's cement industry," she read aloud to her aides as the train drew out of King's Cross, "and with it, Britain's carbon emissions will have fallen by a full 85 percent compared with their level in 1990. That's a milestone that deserves to be celebrated. But we are not going to rest here. I am not going to be happy, and neither should you, until we have borne down on that last 15 percent and can finally say that carbon emissions in Britain are a thing of the past."

Downwood was primarily concerned with setting out a vision of a cleaner future. Her aides, however, were more preoccupied with the questions expected from the accompanying press pack. "There's bound to be one smart-arse," one said. "How are you going to respond if one puts his hand up and asks you: 'what about the carbon emissions from cement we're now going to have to import?'"

"Oh, gosh, yes, I guess there will be one of those," said Downwood. "What do you we say? What *can* we say?"

Several counties flew past as the prime minister's team discussed this problem.

"It's understandable, I suppose, that the redundant workers are going to be upset," said one aide.

Downwood replied: "But they don't have to deal with the challenge that I do, which is to ensure that Britain meets its legal obligation to reduce UK carbon emissions to zero. I wish more people would understand how damned difficult it is."

"But that doesn't answer the question, does it?"

"No, of course, it won't. So what, then?"

"Should you say: 'overseas emissions aren't important. They are beyond our control. It's British emissions we are counting – so imported cement doesn't come into it'?"

"No, too dismissive."

"How about: 'yes, of course carbon emissions from imported cement are an issue, and it's something we are working on.'"

"But what if they then ask *how* we are working on it?"

"Prime minister, can I suggest something along these lines? You say: 'yes, of course you are right to bring up that question. And I want to assure you how much effort we are putting into reducing the use of cement. Construction of new buildings has fallen 25 percent in the past 10 years. Road construction has ceased altogether. There will be no more airports. Our demand for cement is falling year on year, so while yes, it is true that for a little time yet we will be importing cement, that shouldn't detract from the very real achievement we have made in eliminating the British cement industry.'"

"Exactly. That's brilliant."

The whole team agreed, and Downwood committed to remembering her prepared lines. She never got to deliver them, though, because she never reached the cement works.

On arrival at Lincoln railway station, she was assailed by reporters on the platform. News had just broken of a report published in the liberal newspaper *The Progressive*, alleging the government's figures on UK carbon emissions had been manipulated to make them look better than they were. In reality, they had not fallen by 50 percent, let alone 85 percent. Leaked documents revealed that some emissions had not been counted at all and carbon emissions spewed out on the other side of the world in the cause of making goods for British consumers had not been included. Even some domestic emissions had been left out. When, for example, the UK cattle industry was wound down, some people, unable to bear the sight of animals being slaughtered, had offered to take them on as pets. These cows were no longer producing milk or meat for human consumption, but they were still belching methane into the atmosphere – the very problem that led to the livestock industry being phased out in the first place. Yet the emissions from their farting and belching had been recorded as zero.

"It's there in black and white," said a reporter. "Is that not solid evidence that your government has been systematically under-reporting carbon emissions for years?"

Later that afternoon, after a scrambled enquiry at the Department for the Climate Apocalypse, Downwood was able to give some kind of reply. It had all been a terrible error, she told reporters as she arrived back at King's Cross. The 'zero' written in the column, she explained, meant 'zero data'. Nobody knew how many people were keeping cows as pets, nor how much methane they were emitting. Neither could it be estimated, because no-one knew what kind of diet they were being fed nor how their intestines were responding to that. But 'zero data' had been mistakenly taken to mean zero emissions, and so the belching pet cattle had been left out of the equation altogether.

But it was all too late and unconvincing. What went out on the television news that evening was a red-faced Downwood on the platform at

Lincoln station, angrily telling reporters: "That's not what we're here today to discuss. We're here to celebrate the closure of the last cement works in Britain, and it is about time you in the press started to get onside with a government that is trying its hardest to tackle the biggest emergency this country has ever faced."

The headlines made painful reading at Number 10 the following day. "Government Fails to Answer Accusations of Carbon Accounting Fraud," read the headline of *The Progressive*. "PM Erupts over Farting Cows," read the front page of the *Daily Torrent*.

The mood at prime minister's questions was restive. "This prime minister has been caught red-handed, red-faced," said Jake Raglan. "People are dying because we're still emitting greenhouse gases, and all she can do is descend into an orgy of self-justification. It's time she read the writing on the wall and resigned."

Downwood, who had never had the greatest presence in the Commons, seemed diminished as she attempted to make her apologies against a backdrop of constant barracking from the other side of the House. Her own side listened in silence.

"I'm truly devastated by the errors we have made and how it has made us appear to be cheating," she said, her hands white and trembling as she gripped the despatch box. "I assure you, from the bottom of my heart, that there was no intention to deceive and that these figures will be corrected as soon as possible. Unfortunately, this means that we cannot yet claim that emissions have fallen by 85 percent compared to their 1990 level. This little hiccup reminds us of just how much work we have yet to do. But look what we *have* achieved. We've closed the steel industry. We've closed the cement industry. Road traffic is down by 70 percent. Air traffic down 90 percent. This is a very real record of achievement."

"It's pitiful!" shouted Raglan. "Why are we still emitting carbon at all?"

Downwood continued. "To underline how seriously we are taking this, I am today renaming the Department for the Climate Apocalypse, which is now the Department for Climate Armageddon."

Her backbench MPs, who had been hugely supportive on such

occasions in the past, were muted in their response, and some refused to cheer at all.

"Is Armageddon really worse than apocalypse?" asked one.

"Dunno," said the MP sitting next to him. "I'm not a biblical scholar."

If the atmosphere in the Commons was dispiriting for Downwood, it was nothing compared with the mood at an emergency meeting of the citizens' cabinet, held later that afternoon.

It became clear very early on that Evie Wilks and her colleagues would accept nothing less than Downwood's resignation.

"Don't you dare try to wriggle out of this one," said Wilks. "How do you think we feel, having been led along by your merry dance, only to find you've been fiddling the figures? You're out. We're withdrawing our support from your government right now, and we'll make hell for you if you don't resign."

Downwood tried to resist. She thought about it overnight. But she knew all was lost. The crowds rattling the gates of Downing Street were too large. She was besieged, and the entire nation could see that she was besieged. Worse, people on Mob were beginning to demand that Downwood be prosecuted for climate change denial, on the grounds that her government's figures were underplaying the situation.

"I don't understand it. What more could I have done?" she asked her aides, but they were no longer listening. Another meeting of the citizens' cabinet was convened and the terms set for Downwood's departure. There would have to be a general election soon, that was clear, but in the meantime the citizens' cabinet would form an emergency government. A target would be set for cutting carbon emissions to zero within six months – with some allowances made for members of the citizens' cabinet and other climate influencers while they were on business. For everyone else, it would become an imprisonable offence to be caught producing any carbon dioxide at all – although thanks to an intervention from a junior civil servant who had noticed a snag, a clause was written into the legislation allowing an exemption for natural respiration.

Following an assessment of the experiment in community farms, a programme for the collectivisation of agriculture would be set in motion.

Factories and workshops would follow. Eventually, the mini manifesto presented by the citizens' cabinet suggested, society would be broken down into units of no more than 300 people each.

There were some more immediate measures, too. In recognition of the huge contribution made by the young in fighting the climate Armageddon, the voting age would be lowered to 10.

This move made anyone over 10 eligible to sit in parliament and even to become a government minister. While Wilks herself had been intending to take the post of prime minister, she had inadvertently opened the way for a figure who had become far more popular than her, and who very rapidly became the subject of a popular campaign.

"We want Misha! We want Misha!" came the cries from the crowds at the Huddle for Love camp.

"Go for it, my little heroine," Zoe Fluff messaged her followers on Mob. "If anyone can save us now, it's you!"

Sensing the strength of the pro-Misha campaign, and not willing to be left behind, even the *Daily Torrent* joined in, running the headline: "Could Misha Save the World?"

Misha was reluctant at first, thinking she would like to go back to her old life. But the more she thought about it, the more she came to think that perhaps it was her destiny to lead the country. If people think I can save the world, then I should at least give it my best shot, she told herself, reclining in her sedan chair as she was conveyed to Downing Street for a meeting.

Wilks was taken aback by this turn of events, but there was very little she could do, except hope to influence her protégé from the sidelines. The deal was done. Elections would be called, when convenient, when the fight against climate Armageddon was a little closer to being won. In the meantime, Misha would serve as interim prime minister.

"She's almost royalty herself," said one onlooker as Misha's sedan chair entered the precincts of Buckingham Palace. "I shouldn't wonder if they feel a bit intimidated in there".

15

The day that Misha took over as prime minister happened to coincide with Bryan Geavis' first public appointment in his new role as an ambassador for the fight against climate Armageddon. It had been arranged that he would travel to London to pay penance for his crimes before an audience of children in Trafalgar Square, delivering a speech which would have to be approved by the citizens' cabinet.

Unexpectedly, he had enjoyed his first week at the community farm. This was not because he believed he was doing much useful work. He didn't know much about farming but he was pretty sure that the methods being used were not especially effective. He spent much of his days trying to hack at hard ground with a pickaxe. When he complained to his foreman, he was told that if the ground was hard, that was because it had been compacted by continuous use of heavy machinery. Now the land was to be worked solely and lovingly by human hand, it would recover and produce bountiful quantities of nutritious food.

Next day, heavy rain began to fall and the fields turned to quagmire. Would there be much of a harvest come autumn? Geavis doubted it.

Geavis feel he was not being properly financially rewarded for his long days of hard labour. "Aren't I supposed to be paid a living wage?" he asked. No, came the reply. He was working there as part of a rehabilitation scheme – the farm was being paid by the government to work with offenders.

"You should find it rewarding enough just to be out on the land, communing with nature," said the foreman. "That's why everyone's here."

There was no luxury. Geavis' accommodation was a ropey old mattress thrown across the floor of a battered caravan – though he was promised that one day, his team would build themselves yurts. The food could be tasty at times, but it gave him wind. He felt his stomach go up and down like one of the giant gas holders that were a familiar sight in the towns of his youth.

No, what Geavis enjoyed about the experience was the camaraderie. For the first half day on the farm he shunned the other workers, believing them to be convicted criminals. Violent offenders and axes didn't mix, he told himself. But come the afternoon, his appetite for human company grew. He started to speak to the other workers and found that, while there were a few recently released offenders, many were redundant workers from the just-closed cement works down the road.

For the first time since he had worked on the oil rigs, he enjoyed workmen's banter. When the former cement workers learned who he was, they laughed. One of them clapped him on the back and said, "I guess we're all climate criminals together!"

Geavis, who could not stop himself thinking about such things in spite of having vowed to keep quiet in public, thought it a waste that the cement works had been closed.

"If we could only build a barrage across the Thames Estuary, we'd do away with the threat of flooding," he told a group of his fellow workers during a tea break. He wondered whom he could trust, though, when one of the cement workers raised his eyebrows.

"Christ, man! And drown even more seabirds? I thought you'd be a bit wiser after being convicted of ecocide."

Geavis shuddered. No, he really would have to keep his thoughts on the climate to himself.

*

A fortnight after his move to Lincolnshire, Geavis took an early train from Lincoln to London, to give himself sufficient time to make an extra journey out to Essex and visit his former home for the final time and collect a few small possessions – those which his creditors had decided were too insignificant to be auctioned along with the property.

To his delight, he found his thermometers and rain gauge untouched in the rear garden. He would take them back to the farm and start making weather records again. He wondered how the climate in Lincolnshire would differ from Essex. About three-quarters of a degree colder, averaged throughout the year, he reckoned, with about the same amount of rainfall. He could continue, too, to conduct his own measurements of climate change – something he had come to regard as important to his sanity.

He was disappointed to see that his tenants had let the roses run away with themselves, which gave the whole property an unkempt feel. He couldn't take them, but he took the trouble to tidy them up. He couldn't bear to pass his home onto a new owner in a rundown state, even if he suspected the buyers would soon grub up his cherished roses.

Before catching the train back into London, he took the walk down to the seafront that he had taken on the night of the storm. How close these streets had come to inundation, he told himself. Had the waters risen just a few more inches, it would have been so different – the bungalows would have been overcome and he would have been lauded for saving lives. How small seemed the gap between heroism and villainy.

Geavis was met at the station in London by Firkin and a small party who introduced themselves as the secretariat of the Huddle for Love movement. They escorted him to Trafalgar Square. Firkin, it turned out, had already written him a speech.

"Do read through it and say if there are any changes you want to make," said Firkin. "We'll give them due consideration."

Geavis took the sheet of paper, a little reluctantly. He asked himself – did it matter what he said? It was not going to be coming from him, not really – everyone would surely know that he was merely fulfilling his duty under the terms of his sentence. It would be better if he did not even to try to say what he really thought. But still, he was inclined to read through the speech before delivering it, just to give himself advance warning of what he was going to have to say.

"I know I cannot put right the devastation I have caused the Earth," read one passage. "I know the deep pain I have caused. If I could put back into a bottle the damage I have caused, believe me, I would. If I could bring back the futures I have stolen from you, I would. I know I can't do any of those things. But the one thing I can do is accept what I have done and beg others not to take the route that I did."

Could he bear to read out these words? He didn't know.

What about the lives saved through fossil fuels, he asked himself, the human misery that had been avoided through having cheap energy, which had so transformed the quality of life for the human population? What about the people who had been fed, clothed and kept warm by the industries sustained by coal and oil? But it was hardly worth asking even for an oblique reference to this to be inserted into the speech. He knew these had become heretical thoughts. His failure to recognise this soon enough was the very reason that he was in this position. So he kept quiet.

"No, nothing to add," he said feebly.

As he was led out to the crowds in Trafalgar Square, Geavis imagined he was being led to a public execution. He tried to distract himself. It was a day of prodigious warmth for the time of the year; just how warm he tried to estimate. Twenty, 21 Celsius? One boy had evidently managed to convince himself it was rather hotter than that and was in a state of panic. "Oh God, it's so hot, I'm going to die!" he called out, gasping, as his friends loosened his clothing and searched for someone with first aid skills. "I can feel my blood starting literally to boil!"

Geavis was led onto a platform, which had been erected close to the Pinnacle of National Grieving – the stone pillar previously known as Nelson's Column. He learned that he was just the warm-up act. After he had made his speech, the new prime minister would address the nation for the first time.

As the timetable for the afternoon was explained to him, his mind drifted and he started to estimate the size of the crowd. He did so by trying to divide it into groups of 100, creating in his mind squares of people 10 deep and 10 wide. He eventually came up with a figure of 140,000.

Though he did not know it, among them was his granddaughter Amber, accompanied by her mother and father but not her grandmother, who had decided to take a 'nap' instead – her euphemism for a period of quiet and agonised reflection. Adam and Chloe had been unsure about bringing Amber, but since she had started eating again they felt confident she was

189

on the mend. Amber's psychiatrist had backed their decision, saying: "I think it could be quite cathartic for her to hear her grandfather's apology, but please don't try to meet up with him. That would be too much for her."

A few announcements, a few formalities over, it was time for Geavis to take to the microphone. The crowd fell quiet, in a mood of expectation. A brief thought flashed through his mind: all these people, for me! Then he remembered that Misha would be following him, and perhaps it was her they had come to hear. He didn't even have the pleasure of thinking he had drawn a crowd of his own.

Geavis ruffled his papers and put on his glasses. He could read the words alright, even though his eyes were watering. He didn't feel nervous; he felt nothing at all. He knew the microphone was working, because it had just been tested.

But try as he might, as he looked between the sheet of paper and the great mass of the crowd, as he cleared and re-cleared his throat, as he blinked and composed himself, he could not get a single word out.